D0499981

His Favorites

KATE WALBERT

SCRIBNER

New York   London   Toronto   Sydney   New Delhi

Scribner
An Imprint of Simon & Schuster, Inc.
1230 Avenue of the Americas
New York, NY 10020

First Scribner hardcover edition August 2018

SCRIBNER and design are registered trademarks of The Gale Group, Inc., used under license by Simon & Schuster, Inc., the publisher of this work.

For information about special discounts for bulk purchases, please contact Simon & Schuster Special Sales at 1-866-506-1949 or business@simonandschuster.com.

The Simon & Schuster Speakers Bureau can bring authors to your live event. For more information or to book an event, contact the Simon & Schuster Speakers Bureau at 1-866-248-3049 or visit our website at www.simonspeakers.com.

Interior design by Jill Putorti

Manufactured in the United States of America

10 9 8 7 6 5 4 3 2 1

Library of Congress Cataloging-in-Publication Data is available.

ISBN 978-1-4767-9939-1
ISBN 978-1-4767-9941-4 (ebook)

For Polly

But you may have a past already? The darkest ones come early.

Willa Cather, *My Mortal Enemy*

ONE

This is not a story I've told before. No one would believe me. I mean, *really* believe me. They would get that look and nod. They would ask certain questions that suggested I was somehow culpable or that I was making most of it up out of nothing—just girlish fantasies and daydreams. Hysteria. They would wonder how my actions might have precipitated everything or encouraged everything, especially given why I was at Hawthorne at all. I had a reputation for drama then. I also had an appetite for alcohol and marijuana, as did my parents, although we would have gotten along just fine in our individual clouds of stupor, my parents in the living room and me in my bedroom, until the night I stole and wrecked a golf cart, stoned, with my friends Carly and Stephanie.

Carly and Stephanie were my best friends, Carly a girl from an Italian family who owned mushroom barns in Farmingdale, the stench particularly strong the last weeks of summer, when they opened the doors for some kind of airing out. Carly said her family made a great living in shit, the mushrooms grown and harvested in horse manure, but she could not stand to be anywhere near that smell in late August and so decamped to my house, where we slumped around in my bedroom or on the roof just outside my bedroom window, smoking joints if we had them or listening to the radio or sitting with open tin-foiled record albums beneath our chins, the sun's rays singeing our faces red.

Stephanie lived in the neighborhood, a development on the other side of town from the mushroom barns called Huntington Acres, though the houses were on quarter acres. Ever since middle school, she and I had walked home together from the school bus, watching television in somebody's living room or doing homework, heating frozen pretzels in the oven. Huntington Acres bordered the Huntington Country Club golf course; we had belonged since we moved in—something about ownership and membership—so if it was warm enough, Stephanie and I sat by the club swimming pool or used our roll of red tickets to order a frozen Milky Way or French fries from the snack bar.

On that day, Carly and Stephanie and I baked on our roof for most of the afternoon so that our faces were a little tanned, mostly burned—a look we loved and wanted to show off. We spent some time lip-synching in front of my bedroom mirror, my hairbrushes our microphones, Elton John's *Goodbye Yellow Brick Road* full blast, played repeatedly, especially "All the Young Girls Love Alice," which we didn't quite understand, or at least I didn't, but it seemed portent and relevant and about things so far from where I was that the line itself was like a bridge out.

I sang it again and again—"tender young Alice, they say." Stephanie had stolen something from her parents' liquor cabinet, vodka or gin, that we mixed with orange juice; someone thinking close to dark that we should dress up and head over to the club, that maybe there were some caddies still around, some of the older boys we knew from high school we would see walking behind the men lugging bags of clubs on their shoulders. Or maybe we should sneak into the garage and take a cart, I said.

For years I had humored my mother on the golf course, learning how to play and sometimes accompanying her and her friends for nine holes, eighteen too boring but nine passable if she would let me drive the cart. I liked to zoom up to my mother's lie or mine, slamming on the brakes at the last minute, skidding just a little so she believed I would crush her Titleist four or five, the great drive she'd made from the ladies' tee, the next shot she could almost taste. This would make her laugh. My mother was a woman who liked to laugh.

Suffice it to say I knew my way around the front nine of the Huntington course blindfolded, and also that on Friday nights the keys to the carts were left underneath the cart mats, Saturday mornings exclusively for the men who began to play before the fog burned off the shorn fairways, the grass still wet. You would see them in clusters of threes and fours, shadowy, inky, and hear the whoosh and thwack of their graphite drivers as they hit the ball off the men's tee, graphite drivers all the rage. For months I had been saving to buy one for my father, picturing him unwrapping the new club on Christmas morning every time I slipped Saturday babysitting money into the wallet I kept in my top drawer, Mother agreeing to add to the fund as long as I paid the bulk.

Graphite drivers, she told me, don't grow on trees.

I knew about graphite drivers like I knew about golf carts, like I knew that the keys to the carts were left under the mats for all the men early Saturday mornings. For most of my life, I waked Saturdays to the electric sound of those carts zipping past as the men followed their shots. We were just off the third tee, far enough back that it would take a mulligan to land in our backyard but close enough that it happened from time to time—the rustle of a ball through our huge magnolia, Mother saying oh shit from the back patio, where in good weather she sat reading a novel, her coffee in a thick mug, her pack of cigarettes on the wrought-iron table. Mother an early riser too.

Oh shit, she said, calling me quick to look for the poor man's ball before he considered it lost and zoomed off. One thing my mother hated was a lost ball.

Stephanie was reluctant with this plan, her parents members of the Huntington Club but not members in the way of mine—her parents served on the kinds of committees that considered the long-term health of the various species of trees that grew in what we called the "copse"—the particularly tricky rough bordering the seventh fairway. They diligently explained to the bored other members during monthly meetings the need to increase the dues given the appalling situation regarding the crumbling mortar of the old stone wall that ran the length of Old Stone Wall Road, a situation Mother reported back to me, laughing that Marilyn Farmer then asked with her typical Marilyn Farmer seriousness—wouldn't that make the old stone wall look like a new stone wall? To which Stephanie's father, known as the Colonel, cleared his throat and explained how the stonemasons were known for their ability to replicate the antiquarian ways of the original Italian citizens who arrived from distant shores to Farmingdale to work in the gunpowder mills we could still see dotting the banks of our river, the name of which everyone had difficulty pronouncing and so pronounced in varying ways, ironic, since the word was a Native American word that meant crooked tongue.

"He went on," Mother said. "Endless."

Stephanie's mother we called Barbara the Nurse; she worked in the nurse's office at Farmingdale Elementary and never failed to have licorice or lollipops or Snoopy Band-Aids on hand. That I had over the last year convinced Stephanie to steal their liquor, or to occasionally get high, I considered a personal triumph—as an only child my skills at persuasion honed to such precision that even at fifteen more than one adult advised me to go into law.

But Stephanie was in a mood; she had fought with Barbara the Nurse that afternoon, something about makeup or a forgotten chore—they were those kinds of parents—and given Stephanie's not-quite-right younger brother, Buddy, she had to be the one to do everything perfectly, not just for the Colonel and Barbara the Nurse but for womankind in general. Her mother the kind of woman who tacked up posters of Eleanor Roosevelt and other feel-good early feminists in the Farmingdale Elementary nurse's office; whenever you found yourself there with a fever or a stomachache she would launch into some lecture on female accomplishments, as if feeling lousy at school was a failure of character and she had been hired, in a nursing capacity, to buck you up.

So that day Stephanie arrived at our house pissed, a bottle of gin in her knapsack and a look in her eye. That she had begun to so resemble her mother felt a little unnerving, especially when she pulled out the bottle and smiled.

"Sky rockets in flight," she sang. "Afternoon delight!"

And this is how we got to lip-synching an old Elton John record in my room and the sting of too much time in the sun and somebody's grand idea we should go to the club and check out the caddies, or maybe, and this was me, I know this was me, steal a cart and take a ride, given how the keys were right there for the taking and we were two members out of three.

"My parents wouldn't join if you paid them," Carly said, leaning in toward the mirror to apply her eyeliner in what she called an Egyptian scroll before plastering on the blue eye shadow we had found the weekend before in the 99¢ bin at the head shop in the mall. She looked like an exotic bird, or this is how I remember it, and how later that same eyeliner striped her face in black rivulets as if she were behind bars, the blue eye shadow smeared into bruises.

Dark, or close to dark, one of those late-summer nights when it seems as if the shadows absorb the heat and thicken at dusk, the oppressive humidity of the Eastern Shore, the reminder that beyond all this Farmingdale was boxed in by swamps and ponds and soybean fields left to fallow.

In my memory, fireflies pop here and there against the trees but the trees do not look like trees, more like imitation trees, black construction paper cutout trees as if the whole landscape is impersonating a better landscape, a perfect landscape. It is a moonless night or a night of a new, absent moon: everything waiting for the beginning of something else—pond fountains full blast against the rising din of crickets and peepers and that late-summer whir I've never been able to place, that ominous insect sound at summer's end, an explosion of noise abruptly extinguished. And within all of it the burst and put-put-put of sprinklers.

Now empty of the players in white shorts and collared shirts, spiked shoes. Empty of anyone's mother or father.

Only sounds of nature and maintenance, dark expanses of expertly mowed grass and hills, sand traps banked against shorn greens with ramrod-straight flags dead in the no breeze and still water. The all of it designed for entrapment.

I drive fast—dodging the sprinklers, hilarious, Carly sitting next to me and Stephanie balancing in back, squatting and holding on to the metal braces for the golf bags, her flip-flops tucked in the well near Carly's feet. We are flying, ascending the hill on the seventh hole my mother hates given the nasty dogleg, the immediate rough, the way the hill blocks the copse along the too-narrow fairway.

Too often you were fooled into aiming straight with one of your better irons instead of chipping to the crest; too often you watch as the ball soars over the hill, hoping it might drop to where you picture the green to be, land in the hole or right next to the hole, a short putt, the flag pulled away by the caddie or your partner at just the last minute before the ball plunked into the metal canister, hand in glove, slipping in, really, with such grace you couldn't believe your skill or your luck.

But this will never happen, even for members with handicaps in the single digits. The downward slope of the seventh hole angles such a sharp left, a true dogleg, that the fairway only narrowly banks the thick copse, sycamore and white pine, massive and decades-old trees original to the Huntington estate: some people in town still remember the earlier forests of elm and sugar maple and red oak;

the beech that blocked the sun in the woods' interior, like a black heart bound by the same stone the Italians used to reinforce the old walls from generations before the generations anyone could claim as their own, generations that arrived and imagined this land tamed, beaten into pasture.

The crops died. The people died. The forest grew. The sound the wind, mostly, but on this night silence: a still breeze. We were drunk. School would begin in a few weeks. Tenth grade. We were not yet sixteen. There were fireflies against the black backdrop. This I remember. The entire landscape a stage set. Lights off. No moon. This part I remember. No moon. The bursts of water: laughing. The dead whir of those insects starting then dying then starting again.

Over that hill, the seventh-hole hill, we flew. The trees suddenly there so we flew, we were flying, our weight shifting and our screams, laughing and drunk with it—the heat in our faces from the sun we had all day soaked in—and then that jolt, the jolt of the tilt, the hard left, the sudden tilt, still laughing, Carly screaming my name as if I could do anything but I could not do anything, the cart already tipping as if in slow motion though we were flying, we flew, Stephanie thrown from the back, never clear to me how, so that in my mind's eye I see her not tumbling but something far more beautiful, as if the hard turn, the sudden shift sent her aloft to fly as she flew into that white pine, a pine so stately, so old and wise, my mother blamed the thing for not having the sense to save a child, save Stephanie, to tilt one way or another so that her trajectory, *trajectory* not a word I would ever use but one I heard again and again from first the cops and then the judge and then just regular people who thought it best from here on out to repeat the story for me, as if I weren't there, or as if I needed to be reminded what I had done, because what I had done was kill her. I had killed my best friend.

Had killed, I could tell Master. The pluperfect. Not to be used too often because it will take you out of the story in your flashback, out of the simple past into something too far from it—the distant past, the remembered past, some metaphysical expression of the past I can no longer remember although his point remains—too removed from the scene, he said. A coward's tense. A dodge from describing what actually happened.

So here is what actually happened, what happens still: the scene on its parallel track to now, to me: linear and constant, never passing into past, never speeding into future. The sound of Carly screaming my name, the cart sprung from the release of our weight, Stephanie's trajectory such that she didn't make the dogleg, she hit the rough, she had a bad lie, the worst lie, and always the only light the fireflies brought on by the heat, the only sound Carly's screaming, Stephanie dead at the base of the white pine, at least that, my mother said, instantaneous, Stephanie's legs folded in a way that would have hurt, her eyes still open, looking up like maybe she could see where it was she believed she might be going next, like maybe there is such a thing as God and an afterlife, the cart on its side and Carly screaming.

*   *   *

Farmingdale held fast to its traditions: the Christmas sing-along; the Memorial Day parade with all the old veterans in their woolly, pickled uniforms, medals at breast, driving the fleet of Model T Fords owned by our local Mitchell's Ford, tossing candy to the children lining Main Street who waved little American flags courtesy of the Friends of the Farmingdale Free Library. The kids dove for the candy like beasts, scrambling for Tootsie Pops and Tootsie Rolls and shoving whatever they could in their pockets. Everyone strained to see the Farmingdale High School marching band bring up the rear, the flag twirlers the biggest crowd pleasers, the way the girls launched those flags in the air and caught them in their gloved hands.

Around the Fourth of July, Farmingdale Christ Church held a barbecue and peach festival, church biddies in aprons that read *I'm a Peach!* scooping barbecue to all the former Methodists now Episcopalians gathered on the front lawn, sitting on blankets pouring cheap wine into Dixie cups, every year the same joke made to Father Phillips on his rounds—the bottles were water, Father, promise, until suddenly, wine!

The geraniums in the concrete planters along Main bloomed as if it were June in late August, although by October their stems were too rangy for the Autumn Festival, the last of their red petals crushed to a dusty brown ash on the sidewalks. The Town Council funded pumpkins and gourds and hay bales in a unanimous vote, the October Tableaus on Main, as they were then called, matching the banners strung from the lampposts announcing the Autumn Festival: Farmingdale High gymnasium, hayrides and a corn maze and an afternoon crowning of the Autumn Queen, a pretty senior whose photograph appeared in the local paper wearing a one-of-a-kind crown created by the kindergarten class of Farmingdale Elementary, a garland of brittle leaves around her neck.

That year Farmingdale High canceled the Autumn Festival and anyway, the rain. For weeks afterward, it rained, the rain flooding the golf course, overflowing the artificial ponds and farther east, on the Atlantic shore, eroding the banks held by the newly planted beach grass to wash with each tide back into the sea. After so many days of gray weather and mist and fog, the sun all but disappeared behind clouds so thick people forgot to turn off their headlights or porch lights, as if everyone anticipated someone else lost, a road uncharted.

That year my mother, a beautiful woman given to her own foul play, divorced my father and took up with a much younger man, someone she met at a farmers' market on a trip to Portland. She will move to the West Coast and eventually marry him, adopting and training shelter dogs as service animals, forswearing liquor, pot, and meat in short order.

But I suppose this doesn't answer the question, does it? It's not the story you wanted me to tell.

M aster Aikens was one of those teachers. Everyone called him Master, or sometimes, M. I saw him for the first time in late October, a few weeks after I arrived at Hawthorne, leaning against one of the columns in the portico between the science building and the library, holding court for a group of the boys. I recognized one from my American History seminar, Teddy Pyle, and several who looked like upperclassmen, the juniors and seniors I did not dare speak to the times I followed Lucy and the other girls to watch them play Frisbee in the football field. Master coached varsity squash, and some of the boys were from his team, part of the constant orbit that circled him wherever he seemed to be, laughing, always laughing; Master hilarious, I had heard, and cool, which meant if he walked into a room at Dunewood House, the dorm he proctored, and found boys doing bong hits or shots, he would pretend a sty in his eye or mumble he forgot his glasses and shut the door.

He was handsome, too—his Modern Lit seminar so popular you had to apply to get in, writing a three-paragraph essay on why he should consider you a candidate. The rumor that it didn't hurt if you were pretty to deliver the essay in person I'd heard as well—someone said he liked a nice view in his classroom, above and below the neck.

After that, I would see him in the dining hall at dinner, usually sitting at one of the faculty tables on the far side of that cavernous room, near the back fireplace, fireplaces ubiquitous at Hawthorne—many with mantels carved with the school crest, a horse bound up in what looked like a grapevine. In the faculty section, the teachers and administrators sat at long tables just like our own, families of young children and wives and husbands there too. The single-faculty tables looked livelier, teachers pretending they were alone or at least doing their best to ignore the chaos on the other side of the hall, where a few hundred teenagers shoveled food into their mouths, sloshing drinks and shouting over the clang of silverware on acrylic, dishes stacked onto the racks for the work-study kids to load into the steaming industrial dishwashers.

The whole place rang with sound: ceilings high and walls many windowed, banners listing the names and years of past Hawthorne athletes, scholars, class presidents, in gold, hanging from the ceiling like flags of every nation. These memorials were everywhere, Hawthorne as crowded with the dead as with the living, the names of all the boys killed in battles or boys who had lived into their dotage soldered on the greening copper plaques fixed to all the benches and buildings and bricks, chiseled into paving stones. Even the bronze sculptures on display on the library tables or hallway sideboards mentioned someone: in memory of Matthew Curran, 1920–1945, lost in the Philippines, forever loved, that kind of thing. Everywhere.

Sometimes I would see Master with Charlotte P., a senior, the daughter of a model and a famous actor and a girl you could not miss—her hair almost white, straight and long to her waist. She wore exotic cotton shifts and colorful espadrilles from Majorca, where her mother, everyone knew or rather said they knew, now lived with a painter who had earned his dubious success splattering canvases with blood—cow's blood, pig's blood, his own blood. Her father, the famous actor, had died years before from a drug overdose.

Charlotte P. usually sat with the popular students at one of two popular-student tables, but sometimes she lingered at the salad bar, the trays of offerings like the DMZ between the front and back of the dining hall, the faculty and the students. I would see the two of them there talking shoulder-close, or sometimes just standing together staring as if equally mesmerized by the deviled eggs and cold beets. Then Charlotte P. would brush past him to return to her table, passing unawares all the jittery freshmen paralyzed with their trays, incapable of taking a step toward any group that might not want them.

On weekends I avoided this scene altogether, leaving campus as often as I could, the campus deserted anyway, its open fields empty except for a solitary student trudging toward a dorm or the library, small against the backdrop of the changing North Woods. Unlike most of the other girls at Hawthorne, I was lousy at sports, Title IX, as far as I could tell, never having reached Farmingdale High, whereas it seemed as if every girl at Hawthorne had been in training since birth. On Saturdays, teams gathered in front of the gymnasium to board the buses for away games, their sticks slung over their shoulders like Revolutionary rifles, net bags of balls hoisted on their backs, headbands, wristbands, kneepads, ribbons, jerseys, cleats. I saw them on my way to the weight room—my athletic requirement for the week a pledge I would complete certain rotations on the exercise machines to the best of my ability.

Ability subjective, I argued with myself. *Best* another story.

After logging my time, I walked back across campus to Trumbull, my dormitory, to maybe change and gather homework before retreating to one of the foot trails that wound through the South Woods or to town: a few second-hand shops, a dusty pharmacy, a medical supply store, a dress shoppe and rock shop. I liked to look in the second-hand shop windows at the old-timey displays, a spinning wheel or butter churner or wooden skis, or wander into the pharmacy to read the selection of ancient greeting cards, all the cards yellowing at the corners, their matching envelopes gumless and less than crisp. I would sometimes buy one for my mother I thought would make her laugh. I had promised to write every week, and cards were easy: I could just sign my name and draw a smiley face.

Sundays were a little different. I signed out of Trumbull before most of the other girls on my floor were even awake, heading straight to the Depot, a diner near the train station I had discovered my first weekend at Hawthorne, when I thought I might board a train and run away to somewhere else. At the station I had no idea where somewhere else might be, and no money to get there, but I sat for a time in the waiting room as if on a purposeful mission, or waiting for someone I knew to arrive, thumbing one of the flyers from the flyers' display about what to do in the Berkshires, rereading the sentences as if I could not quite take in all the fabulous options.

To get to the Depot, I walked down Oak past the Good Time package store, then cut through the alley to Carlton, the street along the vast town cemetery's high stone wall, the stone studded with shards of glass as if protecting the dead from the living. Carlton bottomed out at the railroad station, and just beyond was the diner, a greasy spoon that specialized in milk shakes and cheeseburgers, sandwiched between a no-name nail salon and Vinyl Revolution, a used-record store, on a dead end called Minton Court. The milk shakes were served in frosty silver canisters, and you could sit at the counter reading for hours, no one pay-ing any attention, the whole beautiful place mostly quiet except for the low chatter of the other customers and the occasional blast of rock-and-roll from next door.

I had fallen in with the Russian writers, their complicated plots and difficult character names, the dark landscapes and snowy vistas, cold forests of spindly birch, aspen, and granite, drawing rooms draped in rugs and tapestries and intricate needlework cushions surrounding the samovars, always the samovars, brokenhearted czarinas drawing cup after cup as their tragedies accumulated like so many pearls on a string, one after the other, polished with age to a sheen or stored away in black velvet. In the thick of the nineteenth century, the endless Sunday dissolved. I would look up to see the light shifting to afternoon.

Anyway, some time near December break—a return home I dreaded given how quickly everything had fallen apart without me, or because of me, I suppose, my father gone and my mother's constant chatter about a new "friend" she had met on her trip to Portland—I heard a familiar laugh and looked up to see Master and Charlotte P. in a booth against one of the dirty Depot windows. The two both familiar and strange, too glamorous in the weak winter light coming through the smeared window, as if lost sophisticates had somehow found their way to the other side of the tracks—literally—and were now surrounded by what Hawthorne students called Townies, early-morning truck drivers and maintenance workers, employees of the paper mill farther down Oak. They held hands, or sort of, their hands more tangled across the table than held, and they both leaned forward, her knee touching his, or it looked that way, it looked as if her knee might have been pushed up against his. Had they been there the whole time? Did they notice me reading? Had they seen me too?

It was difficult to take my eyes off: their hands, how close they sat, the sun on the remains of their breakfast. She had toast, he something more substantial. Master Aikens and Charlotte P. in the Depot. I held my book up as if reading, pretending to read though shifting between the dregs of my milk shake and the two of them, pretending I was not listening again for the two of them or imagining the two of them. On my plate the crust of my tuna fish sandwich, a pickle, the coleslaw in its little pleated paper cup, potato chip crumbs.

"Does he die in the end?" Master said.

He stood next to me.

"What?" I said.

"Ivan Ilyich. Does he die in the end?"

He gestured toward my book, and I too looked at its cover as if I had no idea what I was reading.

"Maybe there's a plot twist," I said.

"One can always hope," he said.

He had dark brown eyes and a way of staring off into the middle distance, his expression suggesting there was nothing he did not know or could not call up from somewhere deep inside him. We had all heard sketchy details; he wrote poetry or was finishing a novel. He spoke six languages. His grandfather bred snakes and his grandmother worked in a rodeo. Tall tales he cultivated.

Something in his face suggested the absurdity of the scene—the diner, the Sunday morning, the winter weeks ahead—and not just here but everywhere, the glass shards on the top of the high cemetery wall, the bundled after-church families along Carlton, scrubbed children in good clothes, as if only he and I knew that the whole world could change on a dime. Or maybe it was that he seemed as if he could read a person's life on her face, because even then it was clear to me that he was interested in lives, in reading lives, or rather, *seeing* lives, right to the bone. And I knew he saw mine, then; or I guess, I imagined that he did.

That was it: our first meeting. The Depot, a week or so before December break, December, I know, only a few months after I arrived at Hawthorne. I was fifteen. Master Aikens was thirty-four. He told me his age only once, although he used to ask mine all the time. So wise for such a youngster, he'd say when I answered.

A friend once called that Sunday afternoon feeling the Ed Sullivan's. I had the Ed Sullivan's those first months at Hawthorne, waking to my roommate Cynthia's hot pot on the radiator, water boiling for the packet of oatmeal she daily mixed in her camping bowl then rinsed in the bathroom sink down the hall, refusing to go to the dining hall for breakfast but needing the iron for fortification, she said. Her teacups were there too, lined up neatly beneath the plate-glass window Trumbull built some time in the early sixties, during that unfortunate period of architecture that required nothing be at right angles, thick wood plank siding and roofs prone to sprouting vegetation, the two dorms on the other side of South Woods the least popular with the boys and so relegated to the girls. I had inherited Cynthia, who in the weeks since school began and my abrupt arrival to Hawthorne had already been through her first roommate, a girl named Winnie, who almost immediately asked to move out given irreconcilable differences.

Everyone found Cynthia odd; she sang opera and retreated most nights to the Music Center, to an empty practice room where she would sit at a piano and sing, her voice an airy soprano. You could see her through the tiny glass window of the soundproof door, reflected in the long mirror on the wall, oblivious, eyes scrunched in concentration. She had long hair and skin so blemished it practically glowed. At night she put on all sorts of salves and creams and tucked her hair into a shower cap, sleeping with her quilt, its cover a pattern of cat faces, pulled high to her chin like the grandma wolf in "Little Red Riding Hood." She rubbed her hands with lotions as well and wore rubber gloves in a trick, she told me, her grandmother had imparted to her. She talked a lot about her grandmother, a woman from Texas, or maybe Louisiana, who loomed large in Cynthia's life in a way her mother did not. My own grandmothers had died years before I was born, and so the idea of a grandmother imparting wisdom, even if that wisdom was about keeping your hands moisturized through the dry heat of eastern winters, felt exotic.

I too would eventually reject Cynthia. I came from a place none of the other girls had heard of, a place decidedly rural and wrong, the girls on the Hawthorne ladder so far above me they disappeared into the clouds. These girls hated Cynthia, although the ones at the very top, Charlotte P.'s crowd, had no idea who she was—those girls rarely looked down at the rest of us. But the others did, and spent their time taunting her, as if stepping on her face gave them a greater leg up, especially on half-day Wednesdays, when the afternoons stretched endless and dull, the gray, Ethan Frome sky predictably heavy, the ground hoary and brown. Then these girls pitched clods of dirt at our plate-glass window, the wet dirt either stuck to the glass before the next rain or smearing a long streak impossible to clean.

This I woke to every morning as well: the ruined view of the evergreens and tall pines of South Woods. Trumbull and its sister dorm, Sterling, linked to the rest of the Hawthorne campus by a path through the South Woods: a carpet of mucky leaves bordering a creek choked with skunk cabbage and fern. The entire place was quintessential New England, greens and reds and whites: close-shorn playing fields and classroom buildings and boys' dorms with names like Marsh Hall and Baker I, Baker II, MacIntyre House, and Dunewood House. The massive stone dining hall anchored the whole, as did the ivy-covered library with its twin lions. A row of Victorians marked the far end of campus, the intersection of Adams and Grove, where an elaborate wrought-iron gate, left open, welcomed visitors. Here the Headmaster's house, the smallest, had once been an inn for travelers when Adams was a thoroughfare to Boston, or something, and reputedly housed Abraham Lincoln overnight on his famous inaugural lecture tour through the state. Beside it was Admissions Hall, with its veranda and cane rockers, and the Infirmary—each painted a pink so light as to appear lavender at sunset.

In mid-September, Mother and I had pulled off Adams into the wide Admissions driveway, getting out of the car as purposeful students hurried past on the various paths that crisscrossed the wide lawns. Each student the same, carrying a messenger bag or a backpack, head down as if to measure steps. I watched as a pair of girls in jean jackets and long skirts ran toward a couple of boys—they wore collared shirts and ties, their shirttails untucked, and Bermuda shorts in varying colors. On our way here, we had passed a number of pumpkin stands, Mother finally holding off asking whether I thought we should stop for a cider or a donut or even a pumpkin to take to the "other girls," as if I were on my way to a birthday party and this were all a lark.

She wore one of her shifts that were in style at the time, floral, sleeveless, with yellow grosgrain ribbon at the hem and bordering the long zipper up the back. Learning how to make one had been our project in Home Economics the year before, a project I so spectacularly failed my mother insisted on joining me at the Singer, where she and I spent several afternoons cutting and pinning patterns along dotted lines, straight pins clenched in our mouths. I wore a similar shift, chosen to make a good mother-daughter impression, Hawthorne the sole boarding school that had agreed to interview me given this was against protocol—semesters had begun, students had already been admitted. Hawthorne had a unique situation, Mother explained. Someone called abroad at the last minute, a diplomat's daughter, she added. She told Hawthorne I could be there immediately. She told me to make the right impression. We both knew I could not return to Farmingdale High. We both knew I had nowhere else to go. Make the right impression, she said.

Except for intermittent attempts to get me to arrive bearing a gourd, she and I kept the same distance in the car we had kept since what she now euphemistically called the Accident, hardly speaking as we drove toward Hawthorne, near Boston, beautiful country, she said, although neither she nor I had ever been this far north. Our family vacations were to the Virginia shore, renting tiny condos as close to the ocean as we could afford where the proprietors did not mind if you tracked sand or sat on the vinyl couch in a wet bathing suit. At night we went to the Boardwalk for a slice and taffy dessert, saltwater taffy our family favorite; sometimes we even ate taffy for breakfast. And even better if the weather did not comply so we would have an excuse to linger at the honky-tonk shops or the Arcade, my father insisting on winning me something I did not need because the whole point of any vacation, he used to say, was to return with something you did not need. He said this with his vacation beard, his arm looped around my mother's tan shoulders; they were possibly high, or drunk. They liked to take the afternoons off when on vacation, was how they put it, closing the door to the master condo bedroom or finding a happy hour in town.

So on the drive to Hawthorne I stayed quiet, looking out the passenger window, thinking. I did a lot of thinking then, and though I wish I could call it remorse or something more appropriate to what it should have been, to be honest the thinking felt more escape than penitence, a way to disappear into a wide empty expanse—a field in which I could wander alone, or lie down and rest. There I saw nothing that reminded me of who I was or what I had done or the look of Barbara the Nurse at the funeral, the way she marched through that relentless drizzle, grabbed me by the shoulders, and spit.

There are many perspectives to any story, as I have been reminded. So here, then: a different one.

A girl arrives. She walks unsteadily through the heat—after all that rain the Indian summer almost liquid. Her mother walks ahead toward the Admissions Hall, in one of the pink Victorians off Adams. The girl wants to be admitted; her mother wants her to be admitted. Her mother carries a sheaf of papers in an envelope from the girl's high school—the girl is fifteen, a new sophomore.

Maybe you can picture her—she is fifteen in the way that girls are often fifteen, not a particular beauty but pretty enough that people sometimes comment, speaking to her in the language of girls: the root of each word not Latinate or Germanic, she might have told Master, but appearance, appraisal, confirmation. Friends of her parents and their few relatives and people who may have known her as a toddler, or met her as a young child, when her looks only nipped around the edges, would often open with *When did you get so beautiful?*

Then the girl knew to smile and her mother knew to say, She's quite the scholar too, her mother fluent in the language of mothers: the looks of girls tricky to negotiate for mothers. The girl senses this. And besides, she has seen the date book her mother has saved in the attic box marked "Ohio," the boys' names entered in the date book ledger, each sentence recording what transpired—dinner at Foxy's, so fun!—in her mother's looping, practiced hand.

The girl follows her mother up the Victorian's wide steps and through the front door to the cool entryway. A student volunteer greets them as if a maître d' at a restaurant, ushering them into an anteroom, the student volunteer a boy with a large Adam's apple wearing a suit jacket and tie with the school's name and insignia. He looks about the girl's age, maybe a little older. He says his name is Sam and shakes their hands, offering coffee to the mother and a soda to the girl, who says she's fine. The mother wants coffee with just a little sugar. As Sam walks away the mother winks at the girl.

"Cute," she says.

The anteroom has glossy dark wood chairs with the same insignia and an oval brown rug on its otherwise bare floor. Portraits of men sitting in chairs similar to the ones in which the girl and her mother now sit hang on what look like freshly painted walls, a paler shade of the brown of the rug. A portrait of a lone woman stares out from the far end of the room, a small dog in her lap, ankles crossed. Behind her, in the room in which she presumably sat for her portrait, hangs a painting of another man. The girl gets out of her chair to see if the portrait within the portrait is one of the portraits from the room in which they are waiting, her mother gesturing to her to sit back down again, as if they are being watched.

The girl's mother sits very straight, her posture suggesting a childhood of dance, yellow grosgrain ribbon outlining her bare smooth shoulders, her tan arms. She holds her hands in her lap in a way not unlike the woman's hands in the portrait, her lipstick fresh, her ink-black hair pulled into a bun. It is as if the girl and her mother have somehow stepped into a hall of mirrors, the portraits reflecting the room reflecting the portraits, an echo or a maze in which they suddenly find themselves, inescapable.

"Here," Sam says, startling both of them. He stands in the doorway holding a Styrofoam cup, looking from the girl to her mother as if unsure who made the order. The girl does not find him cute at all—he is tall and acned, too thin and stooped in the way of a boy who has grown fast.

"Mine!" the mother says brightly, as if on a tennis court and there is some confusion over who will hit the ball. "Thank you!" she adds as Sam hands her the Styrofoam cup. She takes a quick sip and smiles. "Delicious," she says.

*   *   *

Now October, chillier, foliage in bright reds and yellows and noisy geese honking south in overhead Vs, the girl arrives to stay. Her mother pulls into the parking lot, cigarette in hand, Trumbull looming almost indistinguishable from Sterling, each moss-covered and dank, foundations that weep in certain places, something about inadequately drying during construction or the virulence of the South Woods site.

The dorm accommodation was written on a slip of onionskin paper in the Hawthorne packet the girl and her mother received earlier in the week, along with a separate envelope with the girl's acceptance letter, a paragraph outlined in gold leaf with her full name written in perfect calligraphy, a flourish on its final letter, and the many other forms regarding financial aid, health immunizations, and what to bring (comforter, medications, clothing for winter term, athletic gear, toiletries, stationery for letters home). The packet also contained a waiver that granted the Hawthorne School *in loco parentis*.

The girl's mother signed everything while sitting at their round white Formica kitchen table, a cup of coffee and cigarette within reach, the girl across from her rereading her acceptance letter, slouched in one of the plastic scoop chairs that circled the table, four, although it is only the two of them. (The chairs and the table were purchased years ago to match new kitchen wallpaper—stamped with silver and gold—and white appliances. The girl's mother wanted everything contemporary, she said. Modern. I'm tired of looking at cuckoos, she said, meaning the roosters on the old wallpaper the painters had to scrape off by hand.)

The girl's father is away on business. They have not seen him for many days, the trip extended due to an emergency situation at the Shanghai plant, the girl's mother has explained, but they both know it must be more than this, the girl's father cannot bear to return any more than her mother can bear to stay.

They call him in Shanghai so the girl can tell him the good news and he says it was definitely worth waking up in the middle of the night to hear. Then she gives the telephone to her mother and leaves the kitchen. As a little girl, she used to love to sit at the top of the stairs and listen to her parents talking in the living room, Lulu, her stuffed elephant, in her lap listening too—first her mother's laugh, then her father's laugh. Her father called the family a perfect triumvirate of love.

Now she sits at the top of the stairs and listens to her mother arguing with her father to return. Immediately. This transcontinental phone call alone costing them a fortune. They are broke, and the girl's father worries that if he does not fix the problem at the Shanghai plant he will no longer be employed by the company that also employs many members of the club. There was talk at the club, talk that the club might take legal action, or Stephanie's family, until the Colonel stepped in and said he would not relive any part of his daughter's death.

Given their *situation*, the girl's mother is saying, the news that the girl has been accepted is all the more remarkable for Hawthorne's offer of the Taylor Literary Scholarship, intended for a student who "demonstrates exceptional promise in language arts," she reads. Please, she says to her husband. Come home.

But the Shanghai emergency is not easily resolved. And when the girl's father finally returns, the girl is already gone—Hawthorne having stipulated that if she is to accept her place in the class of 1981 she must arrive as soon as possible and use her Saturdays and Sundays to make up for lost time. Her mother is gone too, or almost; she decides to leave, to start fresh, after the telephone call, slipping her wedding ring and her engagement ring into the plaid zippered bag in which she keeps all her jewelry, the few pieces of any value beyond sentimental, a thin charm bracelet he gave her on the day their daughter was born, the first charm a tiny oval inscribed with the girl's birthday so that when the girl was still just a baby she had called her "my first charm." The indentation on her ring finger still looks like a ring but she imagines it will fade with time.

She informs him of her decision on his return, as they sit in the living room, the girl's mother into several drinks. This her new baseline, he notes, which she disputes but there it is—yet before she says a word, before they get into all the messy rest of it, the arguing and separating and dividing and divorcing, they call the girl on the telephone.

How are you? they ask her. Is it wonderful? Is it great? What are you learning? What are you reading? they ask. And after they hang up, the girl's mother says again how remarkable it is that the scholarship allows their only child to attend a place like the Hawthorne School—and wasn't the whole thing, the whole terrible, horrible, awful thing, ironic? she says. If you sat right down and thought about it, ironic?

The girl's father says he thought she sounded sad on the telephone.

She's pulling your chain, the girl's mother says, taking another sip of her drink and tucking her Kleenex up her sleeve. "She's fine," she says. "She's better than fine."

Someone rapped on our door in the middle of the night, startling both of us out of dreams of home, or at least my dreams were of home, of raging fires, of disasters that felled trees and required superhuman efforts I somehow achieved, the trees lifted off the broken bodies, the strangers and sometimes friends and people I knew but couldn't name restored as if water pooling back to place, a reflection composed again, whole.

We waited to see if it would happen again and it did, although this time harder: declarative more than questioning.

"Who's there?" Cynthia said.

"It's Jenny," Jenny said. We both recognized the voice, a sharp, nasal tone, midwestern, from a suburb outside of Detroit everyone seemed to know meant you were loaded. "Open up."

Cynthia scrambled out of bed and grabbed her terry-cloth robe from where she always left it on the floor, quickly pulling off her rubber gloves and shower cap. In the time we lived together, I don't recall ever seeing her without her clothes on, or even in her underwear. She had a pathological modesty, dressing every morning beneath her blankets as if on a camping trek in Siberia, or carrying her clothes from our room to one of the shower stalls down the hall. She kept her robe on at night until she knew I was asleep—or at least pretending to be asleep—before slipping it to the floor beside her bed, close at hand for emergencies: a fire drill, or a panty raid, or I suppose the situation we find ourselves in now.

She knots the robe sash over her Lanz nightgown and goes to unlock the door—this one of her other quirks. The lock. The rest of the girls in Trumbull move in and out of each other's rooms easily, borrowing clothes, packets of hot cocoa, a curling iron, a hair dryer, a dictionary, but Cynthia worries about theft. She told me early on, before I understood how virulently she was despised by the others, that she believed individual privacy need not be sacrificed for community and that she would always respect my boundaries if I pledged I would do the same, respect her boundaries, a pledge I immediately made, wanting to secure my own boundaries.

Jenny knocks again, harder. "Hurry up," she barks.

"Just a minute," Cynthia says, opening the door, stepping aside. Jenny barges in and flicks on the overhead light, the sudden fluorescence like a dousing of water.

"What is this, Attica?" she says.

Jenny is a sharp blonde who lives on the third floor, a

junior who corners the lead in all the school musicals—on our visit to Hawthorne, the admissions director had urged Mother and me to stay the night to see the back-by-popular-demand reprise of the spring production of *Bye Bye Birdie*. In the dark auditorium, I watched as Jenny stepped down-stage to belt out some plucky love song, her fans a rabid collection of pretty girls in the front row I later recognized as the ones who cartwheeled across South Field after din-ner, their long skirts mushrooming over their heads, toes pointed in Capezios I always thought were just for dance. They held hands or linked arms to skip to the bleachers, the setting sun through their sheer peasant tops—not the fash-ion Stephanie and Carly and I had favored, our polyester blouses with sparkling threads and faux-rabbit-fur jackets a joke here. At curtain call these girls leapt to their feet, applauding like all get-out and shouting Go, Jen!

"She must be popular," my mother whispered. "I bet she's nice," she said. But Jenny was not nice. She lived with Missy H., the two fierce rivals and best friends and part of the crowd that dominated the benches outside the dining hall, often belting musical numbers I had never heard of but everyone else seemed to know by heart. Now it seemed a little fleck of sparkle dust had accidentally drifted into our gloomy room—a glint of gold. Show business. No won-der Cynthia steps aside, fiddling with her robe sash.

"Who are you?" Jenny says to me; in the harsh light I see the brilliant blond is pharmacy-bought, Sun-In.

"I'm new," I say. "I just got here."

Whether Jenny hears me, I'm not sure. She plops down on Cynthia's cat quilt and I know it takes everything Cynthia has not to leap across the room and wrestle Jenny to the floor.

"You've been summoned," Jenny says, looking up at her.

"Me?" Cynthia says. "Really?"

"Yeah," Jenny says. "And we're already running late. And running late only makes it worse."

"I can't," Cynthia says. She stammers it, actually, like a frightened girl, nervous, shaky. But she was more too.

She loved opera. That would be the first thing, what she said or rather apologized for when the housemother, Michelle, eventually ushered me into my room. Hapless Michelle, Hawthorne's foreign exchange coordinator, and her even more hapless husband, Paul, a bookish doctoral candidate studying at one of the liberal arts colleges nearby, Trumbull's houseparents, who lived with their toddler son, Atticus, on the first floor. "Door always open for babysitters!" Michelle's mantra as she led me up Trumbull's stairwell to get me settled, droning on about the rules of the place and all the wonderful Hawthorne traditions I would soon learn and how we were fortunate to get to live in the Hawthorne dorms that represented the sixties era, the rest of Hawthorne built at the turn of the century out of stone and brick, or brought board by board from somewhere else and reconstructed over several acres, its clapboard houses and farmhouses, cottages, even the chapel originally from Providence, purchased for the school by the first Hawthorne in the late 1800s.

I had already heard most of this from Sam, the tour guide. How the name Hawthorne came from the Reverend Jeremiah Hawthorne, minister and abolitionist, distant relation to Nathaniel, second cousin, something, suffragist sympathizer, and Samuel Clemens pen pal. Reverend Hawthorne recognized the need for a more excellent secondary education for his son, Theodore, and magnanimously agreed to open the school's doors to his son's friends. Theodore died young and tragically while abroad, some sort of Brussels altercation. A terrible story, according to Sam, though one for which he had few details. Despite this, Hawthorne kept the original brick house open to educate more boys until so many boys clamored for a spot he decided to move the house, brick by brick, to the edge of the town, where there would be room to expand. The rest is history, Sam said, the original house now Languages—and here he gave a dramatic flourish to point out a mound of ivy in the distance.

Hawthorne, he went on, included a many-acre, state-of-the-art campus, the jewel in the crown that Providence chapel: its high arched windows and hand-honed pews dating back to the eighteenth century, its blue-clothed hymnals and red-clothed Bibles donated by a century of graduating Hawthorne students—somewhat of a Hawthorne tradition, you'll see, he said—so that during Evensong and Sunday services you could open any book and read a Hawthorne name from decades back.

"Wow," my mother said.

"And this," Sam said. We stood in front of a massive stone building. Granite steps led up to wide, blue-painted doors, the railings wrought iron and intricate.

"Behold, le chow house," Sam said.

And over there, he said, pointing to the far side of Grove, the library, its cement lions exact replicas in miniature of the ones guarding the New York Public Library.

"Never seen them," I said.

"Really?" Sam said. "Are you serious?"

I looked at Mother and then down.

"Baltimore is our big city," Mother said, although I had never been to Baltimore, either.

"Funny," Sam said, moving on to point out the upper floors of the library, the classrooms we could not see given that classes were in session behind the rows of small windows barely visible within the trimmed ivy, each conducted seminar-style, which meant students sat around an oval wooden table especially designed for conversation and enlightenment. "She's a great talker," Mother said.

Sam then led us past some boys' dorms, white and blue clapboard houses once homes to the quarry workers from the abandoned quarry up the road, he said, annexed by Hawthorne as it spread over these acres like an aggressive nation-state setting out to conquer the world. Mother laughed.

The Hawthorne School, he said, now occupied most of the houses and fields, as well as what they called the South Woods and the North Woods beyond Grove, the Providence chapel steeple towering over all of it, its Revolutionary bell rumored to have rung with Paul Revere's ride. Or something.

Around this time, I stopped listening; besides, much of the history I had read, Mother insisting I prepare for my interview. Girls were a late sixties addition, Hawthorne keeping up with the Joneses as other schools opened their doors, inviting girls' schools to join boys' schools in one big prep school cotillion.

The first girls of Hawthorne had come from a place started by Theodore's equivalent—call her Molly, who also suffered alone with tutors, although here is where the stories diverged. Her father, a stern disciplinarian, had permitted his daughter the study of Greek and Latin and French so that polyglot Molly went on to be among the first to attend a university, bravely ignoring the men who jeered and told her to go home or back to her needlework, fiery lines of Mary Wollstonecraft etched in her mind.

She could not vote and she could not own property and she had already accepted that she would most likely never marry, but she believed in education and said something to that effect in the faint sentences scrawled in the journals of Polly on permanent display in the glass case in the wide entrance to the Hawthorne library, along with a postcard from a past president to his son with the scrawl "buck up," a senior had vandalized by changing the b to f, but so lightly, and with a pencil, that the ephemera was saved.

Girls were here now, was the point, and I might be too if admitted—I *was* admitted, hurrah—and so I found myself hauling my trunk up the stairwell as Michelle carried the garbage bag Mother had filled with towels and toiletries and the quilt she said I would need for the Massachusetts nights. Our little state of Maryland had one foot in the Union and one in the Confederate. We knew mosquitoes, and days so damp you would need to wring your shirt out. But the frigid nights of Massachusetts we did not know, nor could we even quite imagine.

I followed Michelle down the second-floor hallway—its walls gamely covered with posters, bulletin boards, and announcements of cookie gatherings and midnight study breaks. She pointed out the phone booth before she stopped at a narrow door marked by a small whiteboard with *Cynthia Lives Here* scrawled in a diagonal, a cat face, its whiskers long, in the lower corner. Someone had crossed out the *s* and added *d*, so that it actually read *Cynthia Lived Here*, an ominous sign.

The phone booth I barely noted, although remembering, it seems to contain all the loneliness of that place—like the Hopper paintings we studied in Twentieth Century Art, the diners in their individual halos of light; day and night a single, changeable girl in the glass booth, the receiver pressed to her ear as she placed a collect call and waited for someone to accept, reading as she listened to the rings the Sharpied sentences she already knew by heart: *I love you, Jimmy. Get Me Out. This Place Sucks Eggs.*

Michelle knocked, announcing our arrival, though we both could hear loud singing through the door. I understood only that my roommate's name was Cynthia and that she was from Indiana. There had been some difficulty earlier, so Mother and I had waited for a time in the student lounge outside Michelle's apartment for Michelle to hunt down my room key, Mother impatient to get back on the road before dark, a long drive. When Michelle finally reappeared with the key, Mother said she had to scoot, everything fine, Midwesterners friendly people.

She pushed the hair from my eyes. She said the eccentric Florence Myers, the only person either of us knew who had been to a boarding school and whom we always called the "eccentric Florence Myers," had told her she spent her first weeks hiding in the closet and begging her parents to rescue her, but now she said she would not have traded the boarding school experience for all the tea in China.

"Think of the eccentric Florence Myers if you're down," Mother said. "But you won't be down," she said. "Promise," she said. I hugged her and felt the bones in her back.

"Chin up," she whispered.

I smelled her perfume and cigarettes. I wanted to ask her to take me home. I pushed my thumb into my balled fist and stared down at my Frye boots, a ripe banana yellow covered in pen marks from all the days last year doodling in homeroom at Farmingdale High. I curled my toes. I wanted to feel my own body, tingly and weird, as if at any moment I might dissolve into air or worse, faint. I thought of that children's book in which the bullies steal the girl's doll and all she has to do is say Mother, whisper *Mother*, and from across town Mother appears, alighting in a tree above them, towering over the bullies and commanding them to find all the scattered pieces and put the doll back together. The bullies do as they're told, sniveling, because the girl's mother has reduced the bullies to sniveling children not worth the girl's or the mother's time.

She made everything right: the doll whole, the bullies defeated. Then she drifted down from her tree perch to present the reconstructed doll to her daughter, who had known all along she would.

I held my mother, again, and wished she would make it right. She could not make it right. She did not make it right. I did not want to be here but I could not be there. Nor could she, I understand now.

She pushed me away and looked at me from an arm's distance. Look at you, she said. So independent, she said. Then she kissed me on the forehead and walked out the door to the parking lot. I sat on my trunk holding my bag of sheets and towels, my quilt in my lap. Michelle had told Mother not to worry. I would be in great hands.

"Why would I worry?" Mother said brightly.

Michelle shrugs and tries the door. Then she unlocks it and pushes it open. Cynthia appears asleep, or lost in thought, or maybe just intently listening to the soaring aria on the record player on her desk, the record player propped on a stack of albums categorized not just alphabetically but also by a kind of rating system known only to Cynthia and not to be touched.

She startles and jumps up, her face a rough, acned red; her eyes initially kind, eager, although they immediately shift when she registers from the look of me that I will probably not be her best friend. Michelle introduces us and explains that I am a late arrival to the semester, all the way from Farmingdale, Maryland, a town, I would quickly learn, no one else had heard of or come from, since most of the Hawthorne students lived with one or the other of their divorced parents in New York City or Boston, or the smarter suburbs just outside those cities. Others came from similarly sophisticated midwestern towns, or Houston or Dallas, and a handful were from exotic places abroad, Rome, Cairo, the modern equivalent of the children of the

Raj, sent by parents who were diplomats or spies or both, fathers who worked for chemical companies or law firms representing Standard Oil.

Cynthia lunges to turn down the record, to take it off, actually, and then carefully slips it back in its sleeve and to its proper place in the stack on her desk.

"Is she your favorite?" Michelle asks.

"She sings like an angel," Cynthia says. An angel? Really?

"Paul is into jazz," Michelle says. "Charlie Parker. The usual suspects. I've never gotten it, really. All sounds like noise to me but I'm jealous of any expertise. I'm afraid Atticus seems to have taken after his father. He's always banging on something." She looks from Cynthia to me as if either one of us would find this interesting.

Michelle was a tool. Or what we called a tool back then: bland, predictable, her hair flipped at the shoulders and held back by a velvet headband too young for her, although she might have been only in her mid-twenties. I saw her rarely after that, during the occasional times around exams when she would set a plate of cookies on the end table outside her front door and we would knock—the door always opened, yes, but to an empty room—and call out thanks. Or in the Trumbull parking lot with the sniveling Atticus, attempting to teach him to ride a bike or drawing hopscotch in chalk.

"Cynthia is an expert in opera," she says then by way of introduction, although any self-respecting fifteen-year-old

really could not come up with a worse way to be intro-
duced. I listened to Aerosmith and Kansas and Boston.

Cynthia sticks out her hand.

"Pleased to meet you," she says.

"Likewise," I say, shaking it.

Michelle apologizes she has to run—Atticus et cetera—
and leaves, the door closing with a click on her way out,
Cynthia locking it before turning back to me and smiling,
her eyes sharp, defensive, as if at any moment I might lunge
at her, her forehead high and shiny with medicated oint-
ment or sweat. She wears a yellow sweatshirt with a huge
face of a tabby cat appliqued on, its whiskers rhinestones,
and green sweatpants. She shrugs, as if she senses I will not
last much longer than the first one, Winnie. Oh well. She
would stay in her little bubble with its music and its tea.
She would be fine. She has a collection of teas, she explains
to me, because no matter where her mother or father traveled—her father a partner in an important law firm with
offices all over the world—they sent a big packet of tea bags
with a description of the tea, or sometimes loose leaves.

"Of what?" I say.

"Of tea," she says.

"Oh, right," I say, as if I know what she means.

She uncorks a silver canister and lets me look at all my
choices.

"Peppermint," I say, because I have never had peppermint tea.

"It's from Dublin," she says, plugging in the hot pot. "Ireland," she says. "My parents stayed in a hotel in a castle and they saw the Book of Kells. Look at this," she says. She has postcards taped to the mirror above her desk, which, in addition to the record player and stack of albums, is lined with all her ointments. She takes a postcard down to show me: a page from the Book of Kells, she explains, pointing to the tiny illustrations of devils hovering around the calligraphy, angels too, she says. It's how they wrote things then, she says. The monks.

"Cool," I say.

"Careful!" she says. I have smudged the ink in returning it to her.

"Sorry," I say.

"It's okay," she says. The hot pot clicks off and she pours the boiling water into one of her cat-face mugs, then she tells me she advises letting the peppermint tea bag steep for at least three minutes because the thing about peppermint tea, she says, is if you do not let it steep at least three minutes the tea will be too weak and then the full peppermint tea taste will not come through.

"That's important," she says. "Plus it has to be made on the boil, as they say in Ireland."

Then she asks me if I need any help unpacking but I have not really brought much and besides, it gives me something to do; I am not quite sure what to do. I look around the room, her side of the room with its postcards taped all over the mirror above the desk cluttered with potions, glass bottles of this and that, a bowl of cotton balls, twee- zers, and other tools I do not recognize, the record player and stack of albums. On the walls are posters of women in various medieval costumes, singing, and the famous one of the tabby cat hanging in there—tabby eyes wide, terri- fied. Cynthia sits on her bed, her cat-face quilt pulled tight, leaning against several pillows and staring at me.

"No thanks," I say.

"Well, let me know," she says. "I'm right here," she says. "Reading," she adds. "It's an excellent book," she says. *"The Loneliness of the Long Distance Runner,"* she says. "It's for Brit Lit," she says. "Have you read it?"

"No."

"It's excellent," she says. "Kinda sad. He's British."

"Okay," I say. "Thanks," I say again.

"How's your tea?" she says.

"Good," I say. "Excellent," I add.

"Told you," she says.

She was something else altogether, Cynthia. And that needs to be known because she will not last long at Haw- thorne, Cynthia, hated by the other girls in Trumbull, the business of the dirt balls smashed against our window and the way, when someone knocked to tell me I had a phone call, they would roll their eyes hearing Cynthia's opera, or if Cynthia said a word, or sometimes just gesturing toward Cynthia to let me know that I did not belong there with her, that I had different powers, a way of understanding the lay of the land. And walking me back toward the telephone booth they might ask, rhetorically, "How can you stand her?" Until eventually I understood that I could not.

"I can't," Cynthia stammers, but Jenny is a girl who has zero tolerance for a stammer.

"It's been decided. You don't have a choice," she says to Cynthia, who looks over at me as if I can help her, but Jenny is having none of that.

"Turn around," she commands, pulling a bandanna from her back jean pocket as Cynthia obliges, hunching over as Jenny wraps the bandanna around Cynthia's eyes and ties it tight. "Let's go," she says to me, pushing Cynthia forward toward the door, the bandanna making her stumble a little. I pick up her slippers and follow—it's cold—handing them to Cynthia when we get to the bottom of the stairwell. Jenny waits next to the exit door, Fat Thomasina right outside, she says, looking out for any Pinkertons, the guards who patrol the campus at night.

Everything about this is against the rules, I know. Only once in a while do the faculty allow breaking curfew, like when the boys decide on a panty raid. It happened one of my first nights at Hawthorne. Boys whooping and hollering their way through the South Woods, screaming and running the hallways of Trumbull and Sterling, their faces covered by ski masks or Halloween masks or contraband, nude and black panty hose, as they barged into the girls' rooms—rummaging through bureaus stealing underwear and bras and running back out again to toss them into the trees of the South Woods, the spindly branches of the young maples and lower boughs of spruce and pine, so that in the morning the South Woods looked rained in hosiery, panties, the girls excused from morning meeting to pick their way through the trees to retrieve what they recognized as theirs, using the stick ends of brooms and mops borrowed from the utility closet to unhook bra straps, to lift stockings snagged on bark, the whole time laughing.

"Leave me alone," Cynthia hisses, turning blindly to me as I offer the slippers. I wonder why she does not just pull off the bandanna and tell all of us to fuck off; why she doesn't just run back upstairs. I wonder why any of us are listening to Jenny. Lucy is here, and Tina Barnes, who is called Tiny Barnes, and Missy H., Jenny's roommate and rival, a girl from Los Angeles with connections in Hollywood she mentions any chance she gets: the six of us waiting in the stairwell for Fat Thomasina to knock two times on the exit door, the signal that the coast is clear so we can go, where? I have no idea. I look at Lucy, a new friend or rather, a girl who has been letting me tag along and sometimes seeks me out to accompany her to the dining hall, or library, but she shakes her head and puts her finger to her lips.

It crosses my mind then to ignore all of them, to shout for the guard or the hapless housemother, Michelle, but then Fat Thomasina knocks twice and Jenny tells everyone to shut up and walk single file behind her and then pushes the exit door slowly open and leads us out. We all follow, as if Jenny is still on a stage and we are her audience not daring to interrupt, or breathe, or cough, or draw attention away from her.

Outside the South Woods and even the dorms feel exotic in the middle-of-the-night dark, the sheen of those plate-glass windows dull, the other girls neutralized in sleep, harmless. The air has turned autumn-crisp, somewhere someone has a fire, the smell smoke and damp leaves, dead leaves. We are in slippers and pajamas, or nightgowns and robes, except for Jenny and Missy H., who wear jeans and sweaters, boots, marking the two of them as the indisputable leaders of this escapade—and not to be challenged.

Jenny hisses to hunch over, to keep low. No one say a word, she says, staring down the length of us—we will get probation if we are caught. Then she takes her place again in the front of the line, Cynthia standing there as if dutifully waiting for Jenny's hands on her back, Jenny's steerage, her head down, blinded.

Carly and I tumbled out of the golf cart as it pitched to its side—we were going fast but not so fast, a soft landing on the plush green fairway, the grass the springy species favored by these courses, aerated by the spikes on the soles of the golfers' shoes and fertilized to a green so bright that even in the dark it glowed. The smell sharp, newly shorn, fresh-turned, wormy dirt and even a certain mist, imagined or real, from the cool spray of the fountain sunk in the man-made pond ahead, somebody's bright idea to blight the algae and discourage geese from building nests on its shores. Flocks of them sometimes wandered off club property into our backyard, where my mother would grab a kitchen pot and wooden spoon and stand on the patio making a racket. My mother hated geese.

Filthy birds, she'd say.

Carly rolled away from the overturned cart and lay flopped on her back. So cool, she said. That was fucking awesome, she said. I'm going to pee my pants. I'm peeing my pants. Jo? she said. Oh my God, she said. That was so cool, she said.

I had the wind knocked out of me: a hollow, scary feeling I knew would resolve only if I stayed calm and waited. I lay on the grass waiting. I wiggled my arms and legs, blinking at the few stars now visible in the pitch-dark, moonless sky. Maybe I made a quick wish on the North Star that the cart would not be too heavy for the three of us to right back onto its wheels and get to the club garage before anyone noticed us or heard Carly's screams, because Carly was suddenly screaming, screaming so loud I wanted to tell her to shut up, that we were going to be in a shitload of trouble already without her freaking out, that if we got back quickly and parked, left the key underneath the mat again, no one would be the wiser, certainly not our parents, maybe only Jon, the half-brain head caddie, whom no one listened to anyway. I had to get her to stop but I could not talk, I could not breathe.

My breath rushed in and I shifted to my elbows to see Carly not so far from me or the overturned cart, Carly halfway down the bank, kneeling over something on the grass I only then recognized as Stephanie, her arm contorted in a funny way out from her body as if she were reaching, the hand twisted back, broken-wristed. I smelled licorice; that smell before you faint. I wanted to tell Carly not to touch her, that I remembered as much as that from my babysitting Red Cross class, that she shouldn't touch her and we should just get help, but I could not speak and so watched as Carly broke the rule. She lifted Stephanie, or wrapped her arms around her, Stephanie's head drooping back as if she were about to try a handspring, her eyes wide open still looking over to me, unblinking, black blood trickling from her nose and out her ears.

Charlotte P. hurried up Carlton along the cemetery's high stone wall, head down, closing in on the turn to Oak, the Good Time package store: her long, almost white hair, her green winter jacket, faded jeans. Master looked as if interested in what I noticed outside, then turned back to me and smiled like we both already found everything amusing. A few gray hairs flecked his temples, a cowlick. A southerner, Abalama, he called it, Birminghanged; a trace of lilt in his voice, the curl of that smile. I was staring. Was I staring?

"I like readers," he said.

It was as if he molded me from clay.

"Thank you," I said, looking out again as if expecting Charlotte P. to return, to pound on the window, shouting, although by now she had disappeared, taken up by the cemetery ghosts, poof.

"You should apply for Modern Lit."

He laughed. "I don't bite," he said.

Didn't he know the rules? Upperclassmen only, and then you were lucky if he accepted you before senior year—you'd see the clique from his fall seminar, the Modernists, sitting in the dining hall together, their Norton anthologies opened before them like Bibles. "I'm a sophomore," I said.

He picked up my book, which I'd set down on the counter next to the plate with the remains of my tuna fish sandwich, the empty milk shake canister.

"I make exceptions," he said. "Taylor Literary Scholar. Pretty good stuff."

He put my book down again, angling it exactly as I'd left it, and touched my arm. "You've got a whole Sunday afternoon to write something convincing, something that will let me know why you're qualified. A secret you wouldn't share with anyone else."

"I don't know," I said.

"I do," he said.

This was the first time a man had spoken to me so directly—I mean a charming man, a handsome man, a man with a lilt in his voice and a way of looking as if anything I said he could not only understand but somehow make more sense of, righting all the shattered objects back on the shelf—my family, my friends. I had felt the leer of men, the slobbery affections. I was not so young or naïve. Mr. J used to drive me home from my regular job babysitting his twins every other Saturday night so hammered he would paw my shoulder and reach to kiss me before I could scramble out of the car and into the house. Mother said to ignore him; the job a regular gig and I would need what she called my pin money once I turned sixteen and drove myself.

He's just an old drunk, she said. Wouldn't hurt a fly.

So I did not really consider Mr. J's lunges anything, or the only experience I'd had before ending up at Hawthorne, a post–high school football game make-out with Donnie Katz, a wrestler and hanger-on who had sucked at my neck, plopping his hand over my breast as if he were the matron who first measured me for a bra at Lord & Taylor, tape ribbon looped around her thick neck. I half expected him to blurt out "B cup."

This was different. This felt like real life. It can happen to a girl. She can be entirely alone on a Sunday morning and then a teacher can say her name.

"Jo," he said. "It's Jo, right? As in Alcott?"

"As in Hadley," I said. "My grandfather," I said. "My parents wanted a boy—they say I was almost as good, only the difference of an *e*."

He smiled, a dimple. He wore a faded Princeton T-shirt and a khaki hunting jacket.

"Well, Madame Tolstoy," he said. "I'll await your application." He zipped the jacket, thick, good for the cold, and pulled an orange hunter's cap out of its pocket. "'Tis the season," he said. "You can never be too careful."

Then he stared at me as if trying to remember something important or think of something else he meant to say before shrugging and turning to walk out.

I watched him leave, the whole way up Carlton as he leaned into the wind. Snow was predicted later, a blizzard other customers were gossiping about, the air colder every time someone opened the door. Later the flurries were so thick you could not see past the length of your arm, campus security looping a line of rope from tree to tree along the path through South Woods so that the girls had something to hold on to walking home from the library or the dining hall. The campus magically beautiful that night: the ivy-covered and white-clapboard buildings, the chapel steeple and Victorians all tiny, diminished, within the frenzy of snow. Older boys, the Frisbee players, clustered along Grove, trying to skitch behind the few cars still braving the slippery road, running up to grab a bumper with their bare hands, whooping and shouting. They rode as far as they could before letting go and tumbling out of the way. Everything dangerous. Everything new.

I would leave the story here—the snow erasing the day so that none of the rest of it ever happened, like when a film gets stuck in a projector, the images consumed, distorted, vanished. All trace gone.

I watch Master walk out of the Depot, no one noticing but me the way the door drifts shut, the weak sound of the bell. Suddenly, a busy Sunday, the older waitress who had chided me for ordering a milk shake at 9:00 A.M.—you're supposed to get one of these *after* church, she said, setting the silver canister on the counter—hurrying to clear tables and seat the customers who crowd the entrance, everyone talking of snow, the *Farmer's Almanac* predictions, furry caterpillars.

Let the film dissolve here, first blackening as heat ignites vellum, then curling as paper will to ash, its stench sharp. Let time stop. Let time rewind. Let me finish *The Death of Ivan Ilyich* and pay the check. Count out the change and leave a good tip, put my napkin next to my plate in the way I've been taught by my mother. Let me walk out before Master and Charlotte P. walk in or let them never have been here. Let me return to campus in time for lunch. Let me see my new friend, Lucy, or write a letter to my father, consulting a thesaurus because my father likes big words. I want my father's attention. I am fifteen. I want forgiveness.

But here the story bends. From here there is never not a day without Master's shadow across my life—a solid bar, a locked turnstile that brings me up short, trapped on the other side of where I thought I was going, the place I once imagined I would be.

Years after Hawthorne, I see Charlotte P. in a New York club, her head shaved and neck tattooed with a dark bar code, as if you could scan her for value. Charlotte P. is the lead singer in a punk band with a forgettable name, one of the punk bands that played around the Lower East Side bars in the late eighties, or I should say the firetraps gussied up as bars, the clubs and salons in tenement basements, the East Village scene before the condos moved in and the Tompkins Square riot. I'd recognized her name on a flyer tacked up in my local bodega and decided to go last minute.

At first I have no idea whether she notices me—most likely not given the bright lights blinding the makeshift stage, an elevated platform where she and the band screech about something really shitty. It would have been the last place she would have expected to see anyone from school; it was the last place I imagined I would be. I had followed her career a little, knew she modeled right after graduation with her mother's agency, then something about cocaine and rehab and cocaine again, her baldness now as much a signature as her almost white hair.

I want to leave almost as soon as I walk in, but I find a table in the back corner, one of twenty or so people listening in the dark. When the houselights come back on at the start of the band's first break, I pretend to read a copy of the *Voice* someone left behind, head down.

"Hi," she says. "Jo, right? I thought I recognized you—Hawthorne."

She lights a cigarette and sits, snapping shut the lighter and blowing smoke out of the side of her mouth. A few people come over to congratulate her—in the harsh houselights there is something clownish about her face, painted up for entertainment and consumption—the tattoo, the purple lipstick, the shaved head rubbed with a kind of lotion that sparkles. She had been so beautiful; once, on cue, the freshman boys applauded when she walked into the Hawthorne dining hall.

"Master's class," I say. "Spring term."

"Right," she says. "Our edufuckation."

She laughs. She has a raw place on her neck, near the tattoo, a hickey or maybe poison ivy. "You mean he didn't screw you too?

"Never mind," she says. "None of my business."

She holds her cigarette like a joint and takes another drag, squinting. She may be high on something, difficult to tell; she has the kind of pale irises, a gray-blue, that shrink the pupils to points more like punctuation than anything soul revealing, eyes that cut off any connection and close the book on the mind. And anyway all the smoke, and the bright lights, casts everything in a commercial glare.

She blows some smoke out. "Just keeping a running tally for the day they bust his ass," she says, then smiles, and when she does she looks like Charlotte P. again, back in his class, when Master praised what she said because he often praised what she said—Charlotte P. the smart girl. Listen to the smart girl, he would say to the boys in the class, and then he and the other boys would laugh as if in on some private joke, all of it confusing—was he laughing at us; was he laughing with us? The boys heard other things in his sentences, clearly, things we could not hear: Master speaking in the language of boys, a language different from our own. We pretended to understand it. We went along.

"How can you stand it, gentlemen?" he said. "Sitting here as the smart girl shows you up as ignoramuses. Utter ignoramuses." He pointed, his finger accusatory, his smirk. "She right there is going to rule the world. This lovely lady is going to be *your* boss, gentlemen. How do you like them apples?"

The boys laughed; we laughed: the idea absurd.

"But are you just going to sit here like a bunch of dolts and let her? Arise, gentlemen! Arise and conquer!"

Then he winked at Charlotte, or at one of the other girls in the class, or sometimes, on certain days, at me, and I don't know about Charlotte or the rest of them but my heart soared and flapped around the room on those days, the boys hunching their shoulders and slouching down in their hard chairs, bested, or humbled. Ha-ha, Aikens, a few would say as the round seminar table shrank to just Master and me.

"Anyway, forget it," she says. "Next subject.

"The band's pretty good, right? Here," she says, handing me a CD. "Our first printing." On the CD cover Charlotte stands in a slip and high heels straddling a manhole cover, her skeleton legs on either side of the metal disk on what looks like a rainy city street, probably somewhere downtown, her eyes outlined in heavy black liner, exaggerated by her baldness and bony shoulders. Behind her, at some distance, about five guys in suits stand, ties askew, shirts untucked. I think of the Hawthorne boys in their Bermudas. One of these guys holds a whip.

"I wanted to call it *Filthy Dirty*, but the band said too slutty," she says.

I turn the CD over as if I might recognize one of the names on the back, and then look at Charlotte P. on the cover again.

"I like that name."

"You do? Really? See I knew I should have insisted."

"Stand your ground," I say.

Charlotte P. rubs her head, her hand shaky. "Sex sells," she says. And then she smiles the more defiant smile I recognize from some of her early magazine ads, Charlotte's beautiful face I sometimes saw while waiting for a dentist appointment or standing in the grocery line.

After I killed Stephanie, Mother and I were pariahs in our town, people we had known forever avoiding us if they happened to see us sitting at Whitman's back lunch counter eating a grilled cheese or a BLT or, for my mother, drinking another mug of black coffee to wash down her cigarette smoke. It was as if she thought if she wrecked herself it would make amends for the sins of her only child. The elders of the country club had swiftly voted us out, personae non gratae, citing some ancient bylaw in the club code of conduct (the CCC) never before invoked—we were also no longer permitted as guests, not that anyone would have invited us or we would have accepted an invitation if they did.

We certainly understood their position. This all happened in that rainy, early September, the rain that eventually took everyone's mind off me, off Stephanie's death, or maybe it was just time passing, everyone on to waterlogged basements and mildew and the ruination of certain crops.

When the sun finally came out, the golfers once again passed by our backyard on their way around the spongy course, inevitably pointing to our house, our magnolia: the house of the girl who drove the cart, or the girl who killed the other girl, or the mother of the girl who drove the cart or killed the other girl.

I imagine the golfers also may have quoted something they had read about Stephanie in one of our local newspapers—Stephanie's life for the weeks after her death launched into the predictable ascendancy of someone at the center of a tragedy: how she had been recording secretary of the Student Council, poised for a run at vice president or even president her sophomore year, how her high grades, her nearly perfect grades, would surely have guaranteed her acceptance to an Ivy League college, how she had always pitched in with her younger brother when Barbara the Nurse had an emergency, and volunteered every summer with the Special Olympics, her brother hoping to win the gold in long jump.

She had a gift, the Colonel reported. She just nurtured, is all, he said. She was born that way, a giver.

It's not that I did not recognize Stephanie in these composites offered by her parents; by Francis Golding, our high school principal; by the tutor who mentored her in chemistry; it's just that they were all so clearly portraits of the kind of girl who *should* be mourned, who *should* be missed given her do-goodness, her smile, her kindness toward others, and not portraits of any actual girl I knew. Certainly not Stephanie, who did all those wonderful things, true, but also had the foulest mouth I ever heard and who, when her early-to-bed parents were fast asleep, would crawl out her second-floor window to sit on the roof, etching the word *help* into her skin with the nib of a pen.

She wrote on her skin with pens and pushpins, once with the point of a pencil so sharp, she told me, it left the word for days: *FAT*.

That she had cheated on her Spanish midterm I wanted to write in to the editor of the local newspaper after the last Profile of a Life Cut Too Short, not for any other reason than to see her there, in print, to get someone else to say her name, someone else to read and know who Stephanie actually was because I missed her so much I could not bear it alone: I wanted the real girl who had disappeared into this other Stephanie, this bullshit Stephanie, this perfect Stephanie. I wanted the real Stephanie back. Or maybe I just wanted Stephanie back again, real.

Some nights I woke to feel her sitting on the end of my bed the way she did when she snuck out. Then she let herself in with the key we hid for emergencies, tiptoeing up the stairs to sit on my feet and apologize and say she would not do it again, promise, promise, promise, but she could not breathe.

I can't breathe, she said. Me hugging her and counting to twelve, slowly, because a twelve-second hug, she told me, is what you need for a panic attack—that or a paper bag, or a joint, which were difficult to come by at 3:00 A.M. I thought of the last time she did this, when I woke to her sitting on my feet saying sorry, sorry, sorry, sorry, sorry, sorry. Sometimes she had to repeat a word a certain number of times. I was in the middle of a deep sleep—drowned and called up through the water but I could not swim, my arms too heavy, the water too dark. When I opened my eyes I could hear her but I just could not reach her—she must have hit her correct number of apologies then because she stopped and lay down next to me, quiet, her hand on my arm.

Thanks, Jo, she said, as if I had done a thing.

The thought of that night now knowing I would be the one to kill her is like an explosion that keeps happening. A bomb dropped again and again. For a long time I could not think of it, or of her, but I imagine my mother thought of nothing else—every time she looked at me, every time she saw a foursome going by, women she might once have joined for a morning round—my mother, unlike me, an athlete, my memory of my childhood studded with the notes she left around the house letting me know her whereabouts—tennis, golf, bowling—she thought of nothing else.

So no wonder she wanted me gone. And no wonder my father seemed to always be away on business—perhaps already aware my mother was making preparations for her own escape as she quickly engineered mine: she lived on cigarettes and black coffee, as if even milk were too wholesome for the likes of her dark soul: a woman her friends could no longer see. On the occasions we found ourselves in town, women I had known all my life were suddenly too distracted or farsighted to notice us in the aisle or at the counter. Mother would call out to them, as if the fact of them hurrying by had more to do with not *seeing* us than *not* seeing us. Master always said it is all in the emphasis.

Anyway the woman, let's call her Linda, would have to stop then and apologize—explaining she was simply in a rush to get here or there, busy *busy*. Yes, the family, she said. Great, *great*, she said. Everyone *busy*. No one ever busier than Linda and her family as my mother chattered on and on through her cigarette, smoke leaking from her nose like a dragon at rest, or a French actress after sex, my mother's wrists skeletal and her shoulder bones angular, like gnawed wings, beneath her thin T-shirt. She now rolled her skirt, I happened to know, at the waist, and applied more makeup than usual, wearing a darker shade of lipstick, like a mistress, or maybe her usual shade just looked darker against her pale skin. I studied her face, her wrists; the way she jiggled one leg as she twirled on the Whitman's counter stool, spilling ashes into the glass ashtray and on her plate—she always ordered dry toast—and sometimes even down her T-shirt. She was a mess.

Well, she would inevitably sum up. You should know that Jo and I are leaving, in case you hadn't heard.

Is that right? Linda would say, in a way that fooled no one, certainly not Marcy, the woman at the register, who overheard multiple variations of this conversation as Mother and I figured things out—what to do next, school impossible, where to go next, Whitman's so far the only option either of us could think of when we needed a break from the house, the four walls crowding in.

Where to? Linda would then say, completing the ruse, and depending on the day and the hour, the flickering of the fly-studded lights above the lunch counter, the kind of lunch counter once ubiquitous in places like Whitman's, those small-town five-and-dimes that displayed fishing tackle in their front bay windows and sold dollar red-flecked turtles in aquarium scum in the basement pets section, parakeets, and hamsters, my mother might answer Montreal, or Toledo, Ohio (the assonance, she said) or San Francisco or Mexico or, oddly, Tampa. She wanted the rumor mill to have more to chew on—she wanted to stuff the rumor mill's mouth, to jam all the places we might have gone, all the lives we might have lived, down the rumor mill's throat.

This is what I understand now, although at the time I admit to feeling a little Christmas flutter of hope when Linda asked, believing, if just until Linda moved on and my mother took another sip of her coffee, gazing out at nothing before turning to me to wink, that maybe she had changed her mind, that maybe she thought it *would* be better if the two of us moved on together instead of going our separate ways, that maybe she actually believed we would travel together; outrun Stephanie's death and my father's insistent absence.

Perhaps we could just pack one of those battered card-board suitcases you see in old movies and go.

I could picture it—Mother with her ink-black hair sitting on the suitcase, me standing next to her waiting for a train to appear, rounding a curve of track in the far distance. The view is nothing but horizon and light, the morning bluish and glorious; a cold you can taste. You see our breath. We are waiting. Mother pulls a crumpled pack of cigarettes from her deep coat pocket, her Virginia Slims or, better, rolling papers and tobacco or a Gauloises, one of the kind the women of the French Resistance sucked on before delivering whatever news they had to deliver to the informant in the middle of a dark wood or at the intersection of busy city streets. They were important then, these women. They had jobs to do that risked their lives. What had their childhoods been? Grammar schools and gardens; country kitchen tables where they watched their mothers or their mothers' cooks knead bread, smashing the dough with red knuckles, stubby fingers—the cook—or ringed ones—the mother—eyes wide, sleepy, or bright with morning exercise. They weren't dullards; they paid attention.

These were girls who saw what was what—hiding behind tapestries or upstairs in their sleigh beds, listening to adults arguing or making love down the hall, their fingers curling the hair that had just begun to grow between their legs, dipping in, lingering, anticipating more. There would be more. There would be something.

D o not live your life in the subjunctive *mood*, Master said, rereading my first paper, an essay on "Thirteen Ways of Looking at a Blackbird" I had predictably titled "Thirteen Ways of Looking at Wallace Stevens." *See me Re This*, he wrote across the top, near my name and his C+, and knowing from the syllabus that his office hours were Tuesday A.M., Dunewood House, 1A, his apartment, here I was, although *apartment* does not quite describe the jury-rigged string of rooms where Master lived. His office was in the back, next to a galley kitchen cut away from what must have been the original farmhouse kitchen, Dunewood House the northern reach of Baker I quad, the heart of the campus and one of six sprawling farmhouses converted to dorms in a ring that bordered the North Woods. Each farmhouse had a front door painted a different color, Dunewood's a school bus yellow, warped wood that opened to a mudroom with a hard bench and coat stand, a steep stair leading to a warren of bedrooms. Fourteen boys total were Master's charges, Dunewoodies or Woodies; every spring juniors who pulled the lowest numbers in the lottery immediately put in to be here with him: the best.

But that morning the Woodies were out at crew or cross-country, or breakfast, the upstairs dead quiet as I sat on the hard bench next to 1A. The entire place smelled of feet and sweat. I stared at the coat stand loaded down with mothy overcoats and sweaters, a jumble of winter clothing to be grabbed at random by boys on their way out; newspapers stacked on the floor beneath it, dust balls. I doubted anyone cleaned here, unlike in Trumbull, where we had regular tidy checks, the neatest rooms earning gold stars that once accumulated amounted to something everyone seemed to want.

I have no idea how long I waited, worrying the folded copy of my essay before the door to 1A opened and somebody brushed by, one of Charlotte P.'s crowd, an upperclassman.

"Next victim," I heard Master call out from within.

To reach his office, I had to first wind through a den—windowless, with a graduate school reading chair and floor lamp and some bookshelves, a stereo, record albums scattered on the floor; that one of the fifties family sitting in a circle staring at the black obelisk; Nancy Sinatra in whipped cream. I would have liked to look at the others, but Master called out to please ignore the mess, a total slob in domestic arts, and to chop-chop. From there I walked down a narrow hallway, past the opened door to his bedroom, or what appeared to be his bedroom, a room that reminded me of my father's bedroom in the residential hotel he moved into after moving out of Huntington Acres. Like Odysseus, he had joked to me, but your mother ain't no Penelope. I had visited him there over December break. I remembered best his money clip on the floor and the jacket of his gray wool suit folded over the back of a metal folding chair, the sense of emptiness.

Here looked the same, or what I glimpsed: a mattress on the floor; sheets patterned in some jungle theme in a jumble; an open trunk that served as a bureau, I suppose, although his clothes were strung around the room. Maybe he too was planning on finding something more permanent, trying to get organized. Getting organized I understood from both my mother and my father, or rather, *trying*, the point—anyway, this I recall: a stack of books; a scuffed floor; fissured walls; that poster of Einstein everyone had—and another at the end of the hallway of a man I would later learn was Evelyn Waugh. "Hurry up, Tolstoy," he was saying. "Come in, come in," he was saying. "Ignore everything," he was saying. "Straight through," he was saying.

He sat at a desk in a rolling chair, legs up, boots up, a window behind him open to one of the shortcut paths to the dining hall—I only later began to think of this as intentional—his smile broad, as if he had never been so happy to see anyone in his life, as if this very moment, this Tuesday morning in January, would rank among the best mornings he would ever recall, now or on his deathbed. He wore a loose flannel shirt and faded jeans. My first thought, or I should say one of my first thoughts, was to tell him to get his boots off the desk.

But I did not say anything, or maybe I did but it was inconsequential. I sat where he gestured, a wooden chair, straight back, uncomfortable, with a rattan seat, the kind of chair you might see at an old kitchen table or in some-body's front yard with a TAKE ME, I'M FREE! sign Scotch-taped to its back. Here too were stacks of books on the floor. Everywhere. Towers of paperbacks and hardcovers, maga-zines and journals. He would later tell me he had no system but could find anything, any title, even in the dark.

"So," he said. "Remind me?" He sat up a little, swinging his legs down as if he had heard my silent injunction.

I creased the essay again.

"Thirteen Ways of Looking at Wallace Stevens," I said. "You hated it," I said.

He reached out. "*Hated* it?" he said. "I wrote that? What a dick." He took the paper and read his own comments, a look on his face as if he had never seen any of it before. Then he put it on his desk and smoothed it out with his hand.

"You should treat your words with more care," he said.

"I'm sorry," I said.

"And never apologize," he said. "What is it with you girls always apologizing? As if everything is your fault—the Fall of Rome, the Crusades, Watergate, we men the cause of every great fuckup in history and you girls the sorry, sorry magpies. Apology parrots. Sorry, sorry, sorry, sorry," he said, his voice falsetto.

He sounded like Stephanie.

"Ah right," he said, leaning in, still reading. "Now I remember. The qualifiers. The sentences that apologize for their own meager existence before they even reach a fucking period. Do not live your life in the subjunctive *mood*," he said, circling something. "Auxiliary verbs are quaint," he said. "Don't be quaint," he said.

"Understand the beauty of a declarative sentence—from the Latin, *declarare*—to make clear, to reveal, to *announce*. In other words, to *state* what you think or believe as fact: without emotion, without qualifiers, with clean punctuation: a period. Do you understand the subjunctive? To write in the subjunctive *mood* is to write out of reality in a cloud of wishes, in a haze of emotion—"

I'm not sure I breathed as he rattled on. It didn't matter. He clearly wanted me as an audience and so I sat, his audience. What was I wearing? I could not tell you.

"Never mind," he finally said. "I can help you."

He took my hand and fumbled his pen between my fingers. Then he cupped my hand with his own in a way that reminded me of my ancient piano teacher Mrs. Kelly's failed attempts to get me to correctly play notes, guiding the nib of the pen to the top of my essay, near where I had

artfully signed my name and written the date, a pledge that
I had obeyed the academic rules, that the ideas expressed
within were mine and mine alone, that I had not lied or
cheated, that I was upholding my standing as an honest
person within the Hawthorne community.

This had all been drilled into me as soon as I arrived:
as a Hawthorne student I had, knowingly or unknowingly,
joined a rarefied community just a little to the side of regular civilian life, a community of exceptional, honest people
who were to be implicitly trusted simply because they had
signed their names and written the date in the upper-right
corners of their papers and tests.

Did I think all this as he laced my fingers and wrote, "I
will not live in the subjunctive mood," across my name and
the date? No. But I find it ironic now.

"Maybe you can write about your friend for the poetry
assignment," he said, still guiding my hand. "The girl who
died." I stared at his hand on mine as if watching a spider
crawl across a blank wall, his hairy fingers.

"Who told you?" I said.

He squeezed my hand just a little.

"I had a cousin who shot himself when we were in high
school. We were very close," he said. "Completely out of
the blue. I had no idea he was sad. He was one day here
and the next day gone. There. A declarative sentence." He
smiled and I felt a certain loosening, a kind of warmth. And
just for a moment I thought I might breathe again, take a

breath again. "Close your eyes, Jo," he said then, and I did, and he leaned in and stroked my face.

I stood too fast, knocking over one of the piles of books. "I'm fine," I said. Or maybe "Never mind." Or probably "Thank you" or "I'm sorry," given my clumsiness and all those books. I knew I had to get out as soon as I could. I would go for a smoke in the Butt Bunker. I would not say a word or maybe I would say something but not today and not tomorrow. I would maybe tell Lucy, or Michelle. I would tell no one. I would forget it. I would go get a late breakfast. I would drop his class. I would do better next time. I would get an A+. I would see if Lucy was around. I would see if she wanted to do bongs before third period. I would skip third period and walk to the Depot. I would avoid him. I would drop his class. I would run away. I would do better next time. I would hide. I would do better next time.

I passed the poster of the raconteur Waugh I did not recognize and the books I had not read hurrying out. I passed a girl I had never spoken to on her way in, brushing past me, Master calling, "Next victim," saying, "Straight back," adding, "Don't look at the mess!"

TWO

I don't know how others reconcile what happened before with what happens now. For me, the past is a cool, dark pond in which I will always stand partially submerged. That's just the way it is.

How Master's letters got by Michelle, or house security—whether he charmed one of the other students into slipping the thin blue envelopes under my door—I cannot tell you. He may have claimed he needed to alert me to some detail about class or a group dinner out—this before cellphones, email, texts—so that the messenger understood the urgency, or maybe she was just excited to be in on the subterfuge: Master's letters a known secret among certain girls.

I found the letters often, folded airmail envelopes, surplus stationery from Master's Madrid days; he'd had a Fulbright. Sometimes on my pillow or underneath the door, once even tucked in a returned assignment. Charlotte P.

may have noticed the blue corner visible in the folded essay Master slid across the seminar table to me. She looked away.

Certain girls knew about Master's letters. Girls who knew about other things: how to get into bars in Boston or clubs in New York City on the weekends; how to fool adults; how to negotiate entire summer months on their own in their parents' city apartments. They had internships for fashion magazines or museums or publishers or weren't working at all, just reading thick books and having sex with the boys returned from their boarding schools, or those boys' older brothers, or uncles, or even, and this is true, fathers. I guess killing Stephanie defined me as one of those girls, her death like a heavy cloak, woolen and wet, its stench making me an easy mark—like Dora Maar alone at her table in that restaurant, slicing her own skin, watching the blood rise and bead.

I slit the first envelope open with a sharp knife, borrowed from Michelle's kitchen, slowly unfolding the page, its lines and lines of sentences so foreign and exotic on that thin paper they might have been written in a different language. The only other letters I receive are goofy cards from my mother, or an occasional note from my father written on hotel stationery. Stephanie had sent me postcards the one summer she went to sleepaway camp in the Smoky Mountains, my name and address decorated with smiley faces and daisies, the news from camp, as she put it, mostly her love of archery and the free candy at canteen.

Master's letters were from a different continent, the words cramped into a tight, barely legible scrawl. I imagined them composed on a tiny desk, in candlelight, in a whisper.

Dear Jo(e), he wrote. *I hope I didn't scare you last week. Please do not say a word about our talk. I felt you could understand my cousin's true absence, how much I miss him. I felt you could understand this in a way no one else can, given everything you have been through. I hope you will forgive me anyway. Please keep this our secret. You will keep this our secret? I can tell you are a secret-keeper. I know you are a secret-keeper. His name was Brian. Funny, it's such an ordinary name but he was anything but ordinary. We spent summers together on a lake in Michigan, canoeing and fishing and swimming out to the point where years ago, a century ago, someone left a totem pole everyone said would bring great luck. We always thought we had great luck because we swam to the point every summer and touched the totem pole, and because our families owned a camp on one of the coves. We were young boys who did not know yet what can happen with luck, how you can run out of luck. I think you know what I mean, Jo.*

It went on. He wrote of how Brian had been a track star, how he competed in the World Games and won some medals, and how the day Brian shot himself his father gathered all of his ribbons and trophies from his room and put them in a box that no one could ever find again and the father refused to ever say where he had hidden them. How

he and Brian were almost exactly the same age, and how
their mothers, who were both sisters and great friends, had
married men everyone thought looked like brothers. They
started their families at the same time and it all worked
out. It had worked out, Master wrote to me. And then it
went terribly wrong.

I have saved all his letters. He wrote of many things
over those months, his Fulbright to Madrid to research the
work of Hubert Sweeney, a forgotten poet and linguist, a
protégé of Gertrude Stein's who died fighting in the Spanish Civil War; the way he walked that city until he wore
out the soles of his shoes. How some day he hoped the
two of us could go there together. How he would take me
to La Latina, the old quarter where the streets zigzagged,
doubling back on themselves and the crooked houses with
their thick doors that hid secret gardens, cobblestone gardens with collections of old clay pots and weeds pushing
up through the cobblestone, but in Madrid, he wrote, even
the weeds are beautiful. They bloom lavender and red. I
would be amazed.

He would show me the cafes and markets and a certain
hotel where we would get a room with windows out to the
streets we would leave open, enjoying the breeze and the
sounds of church bells as we lay on its wide bed, its white
sheets.

He wrote of his childhood, and how his father worked
for an insurance company in Birmingham and his mother

stayed home and how she would make a pineapple upside-down cake on their wedding anniversary because ever since she married his father her life had been sweet and a bit upside-down, and this had always made his father laugh and grab his mother up in some kind of fierce hug, and that he believed, even all these years later, that his parents loved one another in a way he rarely saw in any other parents or people he'd met then or since, and how when his mother died he and his older sisters had wanted to take some of her ashes to the lake in Michigan where for so many years they had spent the summers but his father refused for reasons he could never name and since then, since his mother's death, his father rarely said much even when his sisters and their families gathered everyone together on holidays.

I have not spoken this freely to anyone else before, he wrote.

Thank you for listening, he wrote.

Dear Beautiful, he wrote.

I know I can trust you, he wrote.

I think of you all day, he wrote.

I wonder how you taste, he wrote.

Secret-keeper, he wrote.

Someone once told me memory is just another draft of a story. All of this, you will say, difficult to know for sure, to accurately recall so many years later—how could I see the look of Charlotte P. as she hurried out of the Depot, her almost white hair against the cemetery's high stone wall as if she too were taken up by its ghosts, or the cold breath from the passersby?

Even Hawthorne is unrecognizable, according to reports: one of those capital campaigns having forever altered the campus. A new STEM building in the Baker I quad; a concert hall addition to the Music Center, a student union built from teak and other sustainable sources near Trumbull and Sterling, now converted into low-ranking administrative offices, their troublesome roofs planted with damp-loving ferns so that, from a distance, or at least from Google Earth, they appear to have sunk into the South Woods and decomposed like one of those ancient

Mayan sites indistinguishable from the underbrush; an Olympic swimming pool and indoor ice hockey rink; and, deep in the North Woods, a geodesic dome where students studying environmental science live isolated from the rest of campus as if on a year abroad—a complete biosphere they call Thoreau II.

And *everyone* wants in, said the enthusiastic student who called to ask me for a contribution to another capital campaign. The Hawthorne School recently ranked in the top ten by the gold standard of rankings, she said.

I listen to her spiel and then dutifully ask her what she most appreciated about her education. (The true purpose of the call, she had said when I answered the telephone, was to convey what she most appreciated about her Hawthorne education.)

So, I said. What do you most appreciate about your Hawthorne education?

I am a grown woman sitting at a small kitchen table in a brownstone studio, looking out a back window to my landlord's garden. Earlier, his grandchildren planted bulbs and I called out to them. Nothing more beautiful than children planting bulbs: "Hyacinths!" they answered, and I applauded before pulling down the sash, the air chilly, early spring. Now there's a light rain, good for the bulbs, I think, listening.

My student caller wanted to be sure I first understood that the fiscal year was about to end and that I had not yet contributed to the annual fund; the capital campaign was something else altogether, so that if I was still planning on contributing to the annual fund, which she hoped I was, I could easily contribute to both, many people do, and here she cleared her throat, *most* people do, she added. The years spent at the Hawthorne School invaluable and uniquely formative for its varied alumni.

That they were, I said.

"I suppose the faculty," she says to my question. "They care so much, you know? Like it seems no matter how clueless I am, the faculty can get me excited about any subject. Maybe that's it but then I don't know." She pauses.

"Who do you remember?" she says.

This young woman has clearly been coached—she reminds me of those robotic calls one gets now where the voice, always female, coughs, or pretends to drop the phone and giggles, apologizing. I imagine after this young woman takes off her headphones she will pop a few Adderall and move on to cramming for her AP exams.

"I don't think he's there anymore," I say, although it seems impossible that Hawthorne could exist without him, or without some of the others I sometimes think of— the lovely Ms. Watkins and Madame Renault, the lesbian codirectors of the fledgling women's studies department, funded to celebrate the integration of girls to Hawthorne by a wealthy alum whose mother earned short shrift as a WASP flying military planes in the Second World War.

Too many women share poor Amelia Earhart's fate, said Madame Renault, railing against the denouement of the Second Wave, the pathetic failure of the Equal Rights Amendment: too many brave fliers are now skeletal remains lost on islands swallowed by the rising ocean waters.

They called it the Katharine Grady Women's Studies Department then; now it is the Katharine Grady Gender Studies Department.

Or Monsieur Hoffman, the poor French teacher with the unfortunate luck to include me among his students, or Popeye O'Connell, the long-lived Hawthorne headmaster who strode around campus smoking a pipe and carrying a carved walking stick. He lived with his wife, Gigi, in one of the Victorians off Adams, its lilacs rumored to have been brought home from his stint hunting Nazis in France.

France was also the explanation for O'Connell's nickname for his wife, actually a Margaret, so that everyone said poor O'Connell must have gotten knocked flat by a Kraut tank, his wife about as much a Frenchwoman as Bulldog Jones, the girls' varsity field hockey coach. In my memory she's a coral shade of lipstick, just at the edge of orange, and tight gray curls, a woman who kept a cable cardigan looped over her broad shoulders no matter the season, and dual strands of pearls and reading glasses at her décolletage, buxom. Gigi O'Connell doubled as Popeye's secretary and spent her days sitting at a writing desk in their foyer as if she were in the lobby of a major American corporation. (All roads lead to O'Connell, we would say, referring to the intersection of Grove and Adams as well as the universal belief that no one arrived at or departed Hawthorne without O'Connell knowing everything about them.)

On the day I showed up for my appointment, Gigi took some time to answer my knock. I could wait in the foyer, she said. Her husband was running behind.

I have an appointment, I told her.

It won't be long, she said. She returned to her desk, her scrum of knitting, the click, click, click of looping yarn to needles.

A squirrel scampered up the outside wall, lingering on the windowsill before hurrying up and over the roof, scattering pine needles and gravelly dirt. O'Connell's Doberman, Pershing, lay just outside his office door, its paws crossed beneath its black snout, eyes closed. I sat on one of the ubiquitous hard chairs in the room, my back to the school insignia. On the mantel a clock ticked, its ivory face encased in glass. Outside the buzz of bees in the lilacs—that sweet lilac smell—and the sound of a distant mower as teams on the adjacent fields played scrimmage games.

In Chapman Hall, Master proctored the SAT tests; in the North Woods, where now they keep immaculate barometric records and grow hydroponic kelp, students carted bongs in knapsacks to the clearing.

*   *   *

It is almost the end of the year, almost summer, much later than the opening. I live in a ground-floor single reassigned to me after Cynthia's abrupt departure, our double appropriated by some senior girls suffocating in their triples, or so they convinced Michelle. Master has a master key to Trumbull like all faculty members, he reminds me, but he could also climb through the window at night, after curfew. My casement window opens to the South Woods path, the crunch of boots, of sneakers, what I hear in the morning, girls talking and laughing. I am in the middle of things: foot traffic, commotion, witnesses, but still he shows up drunk, grinning. "Lookee, lookee," he says, knocking on the window. He climbs in saying shh . . . shh . . . and falls with a thud to the floor. The other girls in the hallway surely know and retreat. Surely everyone knows and retreats.

Master crawls on his hands and knees to the edge of my bed, against the wall away from the window, then pulls me down to cup my face with his hands and kiss me so forcefully I fall backward. He has brought rum to mix with the orange juice I keep in the little refrigerator. I have draped the refrigerator with a tapestry, laid out teacups and packets of instant soup and cocoa on top as if on a table. My bed is crowded with stuffed animals, my collection brought from home, LuLu, and Perkins and Squishy-Wish, my two rabbits, laid against my pillow as if taking a rest. They were taking a rest; we were all sleeping. Master knocked on the glass. "Open up," he whispered, so loudly I knew he might wake some other girls. "I want to see your digs."

"You have creatures," Master says, pouring.

"Why do they keep staring? I think they're judging me," he says. I take up LuLu and hold her in my lap, her name from my mispronunciation of *elephant*, *luluphant*, or so Mother said. Mother is moving to Oregon so everything o-u-t, she said. She needed to get her ducks in a row, she said. You need to get your ducks in a row too, she said. I am trying to get my ducks in a row.

We spent the spring break getting our ducks in a row, the house in Huntington Acres selling in a heartbeat, the FOR SALE sign put up, taken down. Voilà, Mother said. We packed boxes in rooms with the shades drawn and the radio turned loud, the kitchen first, the only thing she would miss, Mother said, and then the living room, the dining room, our bedrooms. On our last days together, we drove to the beach to sit on the sand and stare at the waves, the tumble and froth, the tide reaching high, inching closer and closer, a storm somewhere with currents that could break your legs, we heard; a deadly riptide. Behind us the board-walk stretched for several miles, the few tourists walking or bike riding or sitting on benches.

"Are you excited to go back?" she said. "How's school, really?" she said. We have been quiet for a long while. "Have you made any friends?"

"There's Lucy. I told you," I said.

"I don't remember," Mother said.

"She's from New York," I said.

"New Yaawk," Mother said.

"Right," I said.

"Do you ever hear from Carly?" she said. "I thought I saw her once in town but she was across the street. I couldn't tell. Maybe it was just someone who looked like her. You are all changing so quickly anyway."

"No," I said.

"No, what?" she said.

"I never hear from Carly," I said. From time to time I thought of writing to her, telling her about Hawthorne and asking whether Farmingdale High was the same or different, what teachers she had and who her friends were now, but I never did.

"Oh," Mother said.

She brushed the sand from her legs as the wind flapped the flag that warned of currents. Seagulls faced into the wind or dove against it for the chips and crusts left behind. We watched as one dragged an entire pizza box across the blowing sand. We were here impromptu, the weather warmer and Mother having remembered the name of the condominium unit on the beach in Virginia we rented years ago, the three of us. She called ahead; it would be a celebration before I went back to Hawthorne and she moved to Portland, *we* moved to Portland, she corrected. She has found a house with a room I will adore, she promised. I will see for myself in the summer.

She splurged on a suite with a balcony directly facing the sea. I slept on the pullout couch in the living room and after she went to bed when the wind rattled the sliding glass door and the moonlight raked across the cheap furniture, I stood on the balcony and watched the waves, the white ribbons of sea froth that spilled out on the flat, dark sand, brushed at first light so that the tourists would not be disturbed by all the storm left in its wake, the tangled rope and trash, the oil tins and bones.

"But it's good? You like it?" she said.

"It's okay," I said.

I thought of how before I always wished she would take me with her, that one of those stories she told Linda or Nancy or Ellie were actually true and that we would start our new lives together. But our lives were so far apart I could no longer remember what we had even done or said before to one another, what we talked about when we ate dinner at the round Formica table in the old kitchen that drove Mother nuts with its walls of roosters.

"It's okay," I said again.

"You're a funny kid, Jo," she said.

"Ha-ha," I said.

M aster slips my new peasant blouse over my shoulders and covers my face so I cannot see him but I can feel him. He shimmies my jeans past my hips and tightens my belt around my knees. I am on the mattress in his room, the mattress on the floor. This is the first time. You asked about the first time.

He has told me to meet him in his office for a brief consultation, a discussion group with some of the other Moderns given our clear interest in and total lack of understanding as demonstrated by our papers on the work of Wallace Stevens, the subject of his college thesis, the misunderstood intellectual, a man with whom he feels a personal connection: Stevens a late bloomer, a hero in gray. The Stevens–Hubert Sweeney correspondence was his great discovery while in Madrid, and now he is writing a book, a little monograph, he tells the class.

I skip the bleachers and wander toward Dunewood

House as if maybe I *am* just wandering, thinking maybe I *will* just go for a walk. I take the North Woods path, but there he is in his office, waiting, and he waves me in.

He meets me at the 1A door and hangs a sign on the door that says *Gone Fishin'* with a fish with a real hook dangling from its mouth, three-pronged. "Your no-good colleagues have all canceled," he says.

He shuts the door and leads me into the windowless den. I sit on the cat-scratched sofa, my copy of the reading packet in my lap. "The best?" he asks, fiddling with a floor lamp, its bulb flickering. "The Emperor of Ice-Cream," I say, because it is, although I could not say why or what the poem is about, really—*To show how cold she is, and dumb*—just something about the sound of the words. "Of course," he says.

He straightens up, offering a drink from the bar carriage parked next to his television.

"I don't know," I say.

He wears the soft flannel shirt that smells like him; I know the smell from the times lately he has come up behind me and grabbed me around my waist to pull me into him in the middle of the day, in the hallway to my American History seminar, and someone might be there any minute, and all he says is "Boo!"

"Scared?" Master says, holding up a bottle of vodka.

"White Russian," I say.

"Jesus," he says. "How old are you again? Never mind. Okay. Coming up," he says.

He makes me a drink then pours himself a bourbon.

"That's what my father drinks," I say.

"Good man," he says, fingering the ice.

He stares at me then shakes his head, as if to say never mind, or he cannot believe me there, with him. Then he asks what I thought of his letter.

"It's always nice to get mail," I say, a bad joke. Then, "I am sorry about your cousin, Brian."

"I am sorry about your friend, Susan."

"Stephanie," I say, and then I think I might go, stand up and go, until he says, "Of course, Stephanie."

His feet are small, his jeans ripped at the knee. There are tilted paper shades on the few lamps and magazines and books all over the floor.

"Tell me about her," he says. And so I tell him the business of the newspaper articles and how everyone described her in a way I could not recognize and so I felt as if Stephanie, my Stephanie, no one had known but me and this made it worse except maybe what really made it worse was her little brother, Buddy, who was not quite right and whom she loved more than anything and how at the funeral Buddy laughed, a big guffaw, right in the middle of the minister's eulogy and how everyone turned to him to see what was so funny and how Buddy in this goofy necktie, his thin neck, had waved, smiling, showing his yellowy teeth, and how that would have been the best story to tell Stephanie, how that would have made her day, her whole year, to have known that Buddy interrupted the whole goddamn thing, laughing in the middle of Father Phillips's eulogy, but of course she did not see it. I saw it, I tell him. I saw the whole thing.

"I know," Master says.

We finish our first drinks and he pours us more. He says he likes to get to know his favorites and he is sorry the others are not here for lively conversation and good cheer but nevertheless he finds the present company exhilarating.

I ask him about Madrid, I think I ask him about Madrid, at least he is speaking about Madrid, and about how he almost finished his little monograph but had to get back to take care of family business and so left Madrid but swore to return. I am listening but not really understanding his words, closing one eye and then the other to try to bring him more into focus, the room into focus. He tells me he has a brilliant idea, a very brilliant idea—he wants me to hear a certain song I am too young to know but the lyrics are amazing and remind him of me. They could have been written about you, Madame Tolstoy, he says, pointing.

The record player is in his bedroom, where he goes to put the music on, me alone in the front room thinking how I will leave. I will walk straight from here to Trumbull, following a different path through the South Woods I know from wandering and not taking the real one so no one will see me, and once in my room I will lie in my twin bed and shut my eyes tight and I will not say a word. I will wait until morning.

I hear the sound of the needle set on the record and then a song I do not recognize.

"Come listen," he calls from his bedroom. The imperative.

When I stand I feel light-headed and hold on to the cat-scratched arm of the small sofa, shaking my head no but the music is loud.

"Sit here," he says. I stand in the doorway, lean in the doorway. The room wobbles. "Sit next to me," he says. The imperative.

He pats the mattress, the rumpled, jungle-theme sheets. He is waiting for me to sit.

I could not run if I tried but I do not try. I wish I had tried. I breathe in my own breath, hot, and the sheer cloth of the peasant blouse flutters up then settles down on my nose and eyes and lips like a death mask and I am so tired I might fall asleep here.

"Look at you," he says. "Look," he says. The imperative. But I cannot see me. The thing is, I cannot see me. How can I possibly see me?

No one will believe you," he said after I told him to stop, after I told him that I would tell somebody, Ms. Watkins and Madame Renault.

"The dykes?" he said.

"O'Connell," I said.

"You can't be serious," he said.

I could do as I chose to do but he could guarantee that no one would ever believe me, especially O'Connell, for a number of reasons he would rather not enumerate but should be as obvious to me as they were to him. He thought I was smarter than that, he said. Wasn't I smarter than that?

It should be obvious—I should *understand*—my reputation, my record available to anyone who had access, which was everyone, and that besides if I kept my mouth shut, which he advised, he could not only slip in a letter or two that would attest to my excellent character and scholarship, but also volunteer that the unfortunate incident from my past had been reckoned with and buried and that I was a better person for moving on. He could write I had *processed* it. He could guarantee no one would be the wiser. He could also nominate me for House Scholar next year, a get-in-for-free ticket to any Ivy. House Scholars the only names on the shortlist O'Connell submitted to Harvard every fall: your ace in the hole. I am your ace in the hole, he said. Harvard hasn't turned away anyone on O'Connell's list ever. Ever, he said.

Are you fucking kidding me, Jo? Are you fucking out of your mind?

He said this so many times I stopped saying anything back. I sat in the passenger's seat of his car, one of those retooled sports cars you used to see, an Alfa Romeo, green, its chrome headlights shined to mirror reflections, its battered cloth roof hooked to the skeleton frame above our heads. I pressed my hands between my legs and stared at the place on my jeans where I had drawn a series of boxes with a pen, one bigger than the next, box within box within box within box. I knew he was furious. I knew what he could do now. I was not sure what he would do now. I had told no one but Lucy and only Lucy because she finally asked. Still there were girls who knew; there were other girls who knew and other people who knew: This is the way things were.

Lucy said I should go to someone. You could talk to O'Connell, she said. If it were me, I would go straight to the top.

I'll kill myself, Master said. I'll fucking kill myself, he said.

He grabbed my hand and pulled me to him, fumbling with his pants to slip my hand through the slit of his boxers and push my fingers to his hard dick. Then he arched his back and thrust himself up into me, pushing my hand down, kneading himself with my hand as if we were in this together.

I could have pulled my hand away but I did not. I could say I felt too scared but that would not be right. I felt numb. I felt dead. It was only a hand. Maybe the hand did not have that much to do with me. I looked at the Forgotten Park or the parking lot of the Forgotten Park, the bright green birch, crows scavenging a trash barrel, and steeled myself for what would come next even though I knew what would come next, how he would twist and pull my arm, grab my hair with his free hand and pull me down, my face pressed into his penis, his hands on my shoulders and then the back of my head, pushing me into him, my mouth closed to the bone of his dick as he smashed my face into the soft curly hair there and the sour smell of jock-itch spray. I felt the antiseptic revulsion I felt before gagging on nothing but my own spit, before he came in my hair, on my face, pushing me away and covering his eyes with his hands, weeping or laughing, it didn't matter which. I did not say a word.

He zipped up then, starting the car and pushing in the clutch.

Bitch, he said.

I wait nearly an hour in the foyer with Gigi knitting, thinking how I will say it, trying to remember how I will say it, my palms wet and my own sour smell above the lilacs before O'Connell rings a bell to signal Gigi to let me in. She stands and ushers me to his office door and I am in the dark, or near dark, his blinds pulled and the only light a low green-glass lamp on his massive, ornate desk. He walks around from behind to shake my hand.

Miss Hadley, he says. Forgive my tardiness.

I have never been this close to him before nor, I imagine, has he ever considered me at close range—Hawthorne has enough students that the quieter ones remain unknown, the faculty drawn to the boisterous groups of star athletes, or the funny boys with nicknames—Tooter for George Tottingham, that kind of thing; the pretty girls whose movie-star parents and own stellar performances in the school musicals seem to command the faculty's attention and reverence.

Framed diplomas and landscape prints are hung floor to ceiling on the walls, like the pictures I've seen of the Hermitage. All the schools that have given him all the honorary degrees over the years, O'Connell being a scholar of languages, of semiotics, a philosopher and Shakespeare devotee, a learned man whose numerous degrees look like deftly woven carpets of sentences, matted and framed in gold, the most prominent, the most visible, Harvard College '38, somewhat alone in the center of the far wall, lit by a well-placed spotlight, the kind found mounted in museums. Beneath it, on a sideboard, a raccoon preserved through taxidermy, fangs bared, claws the air.

"Rabid," O'Connell says when he sees me noticing.

"That was Pershing's prey," he says, reaching down to stroke the Doberman panting at his side. We look again at the dead raccoon on the sideboard and then move to the soaring portrait of O'Connell's predecessor behind the desk, a man who O'Connell explains now had something to do with the Explorers Club—and do I travel? he asks.

"My mother lives in Oregon."

He nods.

"I mean, she just moved there," I say. "I'm going this summer."

"Spectacular country," he says. "The Wild West."

We look back at the portrait as if waiting for the man who had something to do with the Explorers Club to chime in—he stands at a library globe, his large hand cupping the

Arctic Circle as if it were a breast. He wears breeches and a whip, a leopard skin draped across one shoulder and an owl perched on the other.

"Stop it," O'Connell barks, Pershing licking his balls. "A hot spot," he says, and I have to bite the inside of my mouth not to gag. My throat clenches and the whole thing is suddenly terrifying—the reason I am here in O'Connell's office, this man, a complete stranger and my only confessor because Lucy said he should be and because I do not know how to make it stop because I want it to stop and I do not know how to make it stop. O'Connell leading the congregation in his academic robes at the chapel lectern at the start and close of school holidays, usually with a poem by Yeats, or one of the tragic poets of WWI, poppies in a bleeding field, men calling out for their mothers. Lessons to be learned in words, he tells us. Lessons to be learned by listening, his final booming amen in closing prayers the loudest, bellowed from the back of the pews, the rest of us facing forward to the white crucifix and the chaplain with his pressed white scarf. O'Connell's voice often the last voice we hear before a beginning or an end. He would know what to do, Lucy said.

He would understand.

"I understand," he said. I had finished my story, the story I first practiced in the North Woods, certain lines of which I'd first recited to Master in the car, near that park where he liked to drive us, not such a great distance to get to, its picnic tables scarred and always empty. The Forgotten Park. He had looked at me in the way he looked at me those last weeks, as if perhaps I were speaking one of the many languages I could not learn, hopeless at French, true, but also at Spanish, German, before he turned away, his gaze in the middle distance, as always, only now I saw the creases at his eyes, the way he chewed his lip.

I had practiced these lines so many times, but first to Stephanie in the chapel, lines that now dried and flaked away in my mouth. I spoke to Stephanie more and more these days, usually in the chapel, where I sat on a hard pew, a blue-clothed hymnal in my hands, donated to the school by some man from the class of '29 or '53. In front of me, the solitary white cross in the apex, eye level with the balcony. Only here in the great silence could I still hear her answering me, laughing or saying what I myself could not.

But now I have managed to—I have told O'Connell what I know of Master, what he has done to me, to Charlotte P., I believe, and to others or surely will—a freshman girl, Allison, how Master said she was raised by a single mother and comes from an infamous Boston neighborhood, how she is not your typical Hawthorne girl, no, and so he thought he should show her the ropes, he said.

Please don't let him show Allison the ropes, I say to O'Connell.

My heart beats so hard I can barely hear my own words. I open my eyes to see him at his desk, his predecessor behind him, hand on the Arctic Circle, owl gripping his shoulder with its talons (for wisdom, he had earlier explained, the leopard for bravery).

"Is that all?" he says. I nod.

Outside, a cheer goes up; someone has scored. O'Connell smiles, his eyes disappeared behind his spectacles, and somehow I know then I have been a fool not to insist that Gigi join us, or someone else who might have recorded what he says next.

"Here's the question that's troubling me," he says. "And I want you to answer honestly—to really think about it." He leans back, even farther, his desk chair the kind that hinges at its seat. "I want you to consider the many implications of what you are saying," he says, pulling up suddenly to stare, although his eyes are distorted by the thick glass of his spectacles. O'Connell's glasses his props, the genesis of his nickname, Popeye, thick polished ovals he often held up as having witnessed the atrocities of Fascism, the liberation of death camps, the depravities of the Battle of the Bulge, the translations of Cicero, and so on, and so on, as if everything were contained in his magic spectacles, or everything that mattered.

"Believe me," I say. "I have."

"The seriousness," he says.

"Yes, sir," I say.

He rubs the bridge of his nose. At the time I imagined him a hundred years old, but he may not yet have been seventy—the kind of high forehead and receding hairline that suggests intelligence beyond an ordinary mortal's comprehension.

"You will ruin a man's career," he says. "And here I've been told you are a smart girl."

"That could be argued," I say, wiping my palms on the lap of my dress, a sundress of the kind popular then, a halter top that tied around my neck. I can see myself there in that sundress: its pattern bright yellow sunflowers, its apron skirt and deep pockets. A creation from that Home Economics class Stephanie and I took together, side by side at sewing machines pinning tissue-paper patterns to the fabrics we had picked out the weekend before at Whitman's: Stephanie's windmills, mine sunflowers.

I sit with my ankles crossed as I have been taught to do when wearing a skirt or dress, my bare legs sticky from heat and nerves. I rub the cloth in my lap as if picking the sunflowers bald.

"You must realize how complicated these things are, these kinds of accusations. How ugly they can become, how baroque," he says.

I nod, although I have no idea what *baroque* means in this context.

"For example," he says. "That dress you're wearing."

I feel the heat spread up from my chest, all of me suddenly flushed and wrong, as if burned by the brightness of the yellow, the sun bearing down.

"I made it," I say.

"Nevertheless, it complicates an accusation of this sort when the quote unquote victim chooses to wear a dress with bare shoulders and no brassiere."

I look down.

"What?" O'Connell says. He leans forward, his whiskered face, few strands of oiled hair, his pate, but what he truly looks like I could not say—hidden behind those spectacles as if in a bunker constructed out of all of world history, war his shield, his right and privilege. "I didn't hear you," he says.

"It's the truth," I say.

O'Connell links his fingers together and then waggles them, as if for exercise.

"I know that you have had some problems at home. You came to us from a very difficult situation."

"This isn't about that."

"Nevertheless," he says. "I want you to think it through." He smiles. "You have a lot to look forward to next year. Junior year. And I understand you may be suggested for House Scholar."

"I never asked him to—"

"He mentioned it."

So they had already spoken. I rub at the broadest sunflower in my lap.

"I know this is your version," he says. "But there are always two sides to every story. You understand, for the record, we'll have to hear his. And then we'll have to make our own decision."

What did I want to do? What should I have done? What did I do?

I should have reached across that polished desk with its antique inkwell and granite paperweight—he had mentioned both—to tear those spectacles from his face, drop them to the warped, wooden floor, the threadbare Oriental, and ground the glass into its pattern with my heel, a simple flat from my mother's discard pile for occasions when, as she put it, I needed to *dress*. I should have smashed those spectacles to glass so fine he would never not remember how I ruined his vision—decisive, quick, imperative—and wrecked that world of his own making, its heroes, its scholars, its founding members, generals, politicians, row after row after row after row of men and not real and not true for me, for *me*; not how I was, or what I saw and thought. Not anything. I could have; I should have; I did not.

But I was fifteen. I could no more have formed those words, those thoughts, than flown to the moon. I have reviewed it again and again, all the stories hiding in plain sight: the rape of the swan, the rape of the Sabine; the man who ripped the phone cord from the wall, the hordes on the bus, the crippled girl in the pool room, the servant, the slave. What I might have done; what they could not do; what I did not do.

The past conditional, Master said, like breath in winter, puffs of air, a crystallized white nothingness, pretty to consider but gone with the breeze, empty of sustenance, form, lost between un-being and being, he said, ten points if we could name the poet. "*Caught in the form of limitation / Between un-being and being,*" he wrote on the board, the chalk on his hands so dry. He clapped and sent up a cloud.

"Eliot," someone said, and we moved to other things.

"I have a busy day," O'Connell says, looking down.

And that was it: rage woven into my life with steel thread.

Somehow Gigi stands at the door. O'Connell busying the stack of papers on his heavy desk. Outside crows; the day turned hot, the Doberman sleeping and still. I thank O'Connell for his time, or maybe I just leave.

"Not at all," he says, already distracted.

I turn to Gigi, who smiles, uncharacteristically, lipstick fresh, and asks if I want some lemonade. It's hot and she has just made a pitcher, she says, guiding me out and through the foyer, past her desk and the hard chairs and into what looks like an ordinary kitchen, curtains over the sink and an oval table, where presumably she and O'Connell eat their breakfast each morning, O'Connell reading the international news, all those newspapers splayed around the room, the *Financial Times*, *The Wall Street Journal*, *The New York Times*, as Gigi twirls the Lazy Susan at the center of the oval table, offering from its crowded bounty: honey and cinnamon and sugar and salt and pepper in his-and-her ceramic poodle shakers.

"Aren't those silly?" Gigi says. She pours me a glass. "People think because of that darn Doberman that we are dog fanatics, which we are, I guess, but every year for Christmas you can imagine all the dog gifts. Most of them we give away, but we kind of liked these little guys." She picks up the female, salt. "Woof, woof," she says, laughing. I sit across from her and drink my lemonade. She puts down the poodle saltshaker and reaches for my hand.

"He's set in his ways," she says. "Don't let it bother you. Hard to teach that old dog new tricks," she says. "You'll see. We used to say when I was a little girl at summer camp, 'Make big waves and you'll swamp your own boat.'" Her expression changes, becomes more open, as if maybe the original Margaret, the summer camp Margaret, dressed in the requisite white blouse and bloomers, her arms and legs tanned from all those days in the sun, her eyes bright with fresh air, has just, for an instant, swum to the surface to deliver this message—girl to girl.

I stare at her. Had she been listening at the door? Did she somehow know what I had come to say? Did they all know? But then the doorbell rings and startles us both, the young Margaret disappearing back into the depths as Gigi stands, knocking the poodle to the table, spilling a little salt on the table.

"Oh, no," she says. "Bad luck," she says, scooping up as much as she can and tossing it over her shoulder. "That's better," she says. "Let's go." And so I follow her through the foyer, past her desk, the hard chairs, to the front door, where she lets in another student, an older boy I do not recognize, who rolls his eyes as he passes me—disciplinary. Gigi says something to him as I step out to the veranda. And then she closes the door behind me.

I never finished the story of Cynthia.

There were six girls in total, seven counting her. I can picture the Lanz nightgown, white flannel covered in a cheerful flower print, its high ruffled neck buttoned at the back, a thin thread looped on a pearl—the only things missing a bonnet and candlestick. Early in our weeks as roommates, Cynthia confessed that her mother wore the exact same nightgown back in Indiana; that her mother struggled to loop the same nearly invisible thread around the pearly button every night and that she, Cynthia, found this comforting, although *comforting* was probably not the word she used. Cynthia said she and her mother had been wearing matching nightgowns ever since she could remember.

I imagine Cynthia's mother also washed her face as thoroughly before retiring, careful of the neck ruffle, the elastic at her wrists jammed to her elbows to hold back the billowing, eighteenth-century sleeves. She tries her best, staring down age—wrinkles, gray hair—with creams and dyes, her awkward daughter hundreds of miles from home but in a safe place, a place known for its music program, where surely her daughter might have an easier time making friends?

But Cynthia's mother is nowhere in sight. She has no idea what is happening to her girl now.

We take a shortcut through the South Woods to avoid the path, our feet mucked from the autumn sludge, this before Thanksgiving, everyone already studying for midterms and counting pages to be read and pages to be written. Maybe it was some kind of exam ritual, I thought, falling at the end of the line behind Lucy, who lived on the second floor and had sat next to me at my first Trumbull house meeting.

"Time to lose the hair, Farrah," she said, sitting cross-legged on the carpeted floor of the lounge, a collection of beanbags, a television, and a soda and candy machine. "The eye shadow too."

Lucy was one of the best sophomore athletes at Hawthorne, already a coxswain on the varsity crew team, which basically meant she said anything she pleased, loudly, and knew the drill of what to do and what not to do. She had been at Hawthorne for a year, a family tradition, boarding school, she the first girl to go to Hawthorne, her brothers—four of them—having graduated years before, the youngest and tallest they called Slim at Cornell.

He's *cerebral*, she told me.

Lucy turns now to give me a stern look and gestures for me to hurry. We are thick in the South Woods, following the shortcut I had found on my early weekend wanderings, a separate path that led out to the library. Pinkertons' lights flash in the far distance, one of the guards patrolling Baker I quad, no doubt looking for the usual suspects, the senior boys. We knew the Pinkertons knocked off around 4:00 A.M., when some of the girls, the very early risers like Lucy, would sneak out to the basement of the dining hall where the donut maker, a Vietnam vet named PJ, recited war stories and getting high stories and fed the girls as many donuts as they wanted. Lucy had told me there was nothing better than sitting with PJ as the sun came up eating fresh donuts. She had promised she would take me sometime.

But even though we are near the dining hall, I guess this is not about leading Cynthia blindfolded to the warmth of the basement and donuts.

"Who said something?" Jenny says. She raises her hand and we all stop, trying to blend into the ivy of the library. "Jesus, people," she says. Fat Thomasina is leaning over, her shoulders shaking, laughing.

"Sorry," Fat Thomasina whispers. "Nerves."

A car slows down near the intersection of Grove and Adams, splitting the dark with its headlights. Jenny signals to stay and so we do, barely breathing. I watch the outline of the driver at the wheel, the driver uncertain of something, coasting then speeding up after the stop sign, almost gone before I realize Jenny has lowered her hand and gestured for us to continue. We turn the corner of the library, sprinting past the science building to the sidewalk that borders town, off-campus, the main street of Oak, the only light the blinking neon OPEN of the Good Time package store, even though the store is clearly closed. Someone must have forgotten.

We are single file, silent—Cynthia presumably in the lead, or pushed forward by Jenny. I cannot see from my place behind Lucy. I follow the back of Lucy's head, her tight braid, as we cross Main, its one traffic light blinking yellow as if anyone would pay attention, would comply. No cars. Shops shuttered. Streets empty. In Farmingdale, the Christmas lights would already be looped streetlamp to streetlamp, ready to be lit the day after Thanksgiving. The flagpole too, the one at the small memorial in the town square or, as Stephanie used to say, the town rectangle. And on the obelisk granite monument to the town's war dead, its pink stone etched with names Stephanie and I liked to read aloud, the head of the Shriners would have already placed an evergreen wreath, another Farmingdale tradition Stephanie and I loved, since Christmas was our favorite holiday bar none.

Bar none, we used to say. Bar fucking none, we said about Christmas. We wrote letters to Santa for years, and then Christmas lists for our parents: last year Camaro at the top of hers; Mustang at the top of mine. We had twin visions of driving from one side of the country to the other. Eventually we would turn sixteen.

The OPEN sign blinks on and off as we near the Good Time package store. Like Gatsby's green light, I would have told Stephanie, remembering Miss Lautimore, my old English teacher, as she read the last paragraph aloud about the sound of waves on the shore at the front of the classroom at the end of the day, when we all felt lonely. Fitzgerald misunderstood, she said—the unobtainable first love and all that crap, she said, and we loved that the old lady said *crap* and wore beautiful, elegant shoes and blazers and seemed to have stepped out of a Fitzgerald novel herself, maybe *Tender Is the Night*. I had gone on a little Fitzgerald kick last year and told Stephanie that I thought New York be damned, we needed to hightail it to Paris after college. And because she was Stephanie, she read the book. And because she was Stephanie, she said New York be damned.

Jenny raises her hand and we all stop, circling her where she stands beside Cynthia, her head a little cocked, as if listening to something none of the rest of us can hear.

In case any of you are still wondering, Jenny says, it has come to our attention that our good friend Cynthia has narked about the North Woods, singlehandedly convincing the boys that Trumbull are *losers, capisce?*

"*Capisce,*" Fat Thomasina says. She is always the right-hand man, and seems not to mind her nickname or the fact that she lugs along behind whoever is a notch or two above her on the ladder—Fat Thomasina is even pretty popular with the superpopular girls, the ones who trail Charlotte P. after dinner to the bleachers, or watch when she wanders off alone toward the boys' quads on her way to hang out with one of the seniors she knows in Dunewood House, or Baker II.

I look at Cynthia, who stands as if waiting to be twirled around for a game of pin the tail on the donkey. It is hard to have any idea what she's thinking. In the silence she might be humming.

"Can you gag her mouth?" Fat Thomasina says, but Jenny does not appear to hear, she pushes Cynthia forward again and only now do I understand that we are turning off Oak to Carlton, heading past the cemetery toward the train tracks and the train station.

The cemetery gates are padlocked—people dying to get in! my father would say. Within rows of neat gravestones, miniature American flags shoved into the ground next to vials of plastic flowers or pots of mums, the clutter of the necropolis, a word I would not have thought of that Jenny pronounces as she narrates the direction for Cynthia, her voice monotone, telling Cynthia they are now moving "past the necropolis toward doom."

I know about the North Woods, the kids who get stoned in the clearing, a place Cynthia showed me around the time I arrived, saying she sometimes liked to go there to

practice—the cold, barren piano rooms in the Music Center lousy for inspiration, the clearing far better, she said,
and where the popular girls met Sunday afternoons to get
stoned before vespers, the Gospels funny if you thought
about them that way, Lucy would later say to me in the
same spot, passing a joint I barely lipped before passing it
back again.

The clearing was in the middle of a circle of white pines
so old they had lost their bushy shape and grown massive,
the sound of the wind through their green needles like its
own voice, the smell of the needles that had fallen to the
ground in soft, brown clumps the stoners piled up in winter
and lit on fire. They looked like Fourth of July sparklers as
they fizzled out and burned bright orange to black.

Cynthia always approached from a particular path to
make sure no one else was there—drawn by something
about the acoustics, the ring of thick trunks better and less
depressing than the Music Center with its hallway gallery
of all the druggie art kids' self-portraits, their jagged noses
and Picasso eyes, or eye, she said, laughing. She liked to
practice here until the stoners booted her.

Singing, she explained to me, was unique to all of us,
and did I know that? Did I know that we were the only
animals who could actually sing and speak? That we were
primed for singing, that our ancestors, like cavemen ancestors, sang before they spoke?

She just wished everyone knew it, she said when I told

her I had never heard that before. She just wished everyone knew that because maybe then we would all be singing or singing more or that it wouldn't be weird.

And then she sang something on the opera hit parade—I had never been to an opera, or even a musical outside Hawthorne's *Bye Bye Birdie* production—and her voice filled the whole space, the pocket of space in the middle of the stoner woods, the height of the white pines and the moss at their bumpy roots, so that every time I went back there, even long after Cynthia was gone, I thought I could still hear her, as if the echo of the song had been trapped there for eternity, or maybe just my eternity, given everything.

We reach the train station, closed now, and turn the corner to the platform, a concrete slab lit by a single bulb, a bench. Jenny pushes Cynthia up to the platform, next to where the tracks cross the street, and takes her by her shoulders.

"Do you admit to your crime, Nark?" she says.

Cynthia nods.

"What did she say?" Tiny Barnes says. She can barely see anything, she says. But then, none of us can see much, the only light from that solitary bulb, the buildings nearby just slanting shadows.

"Shut up," Lucy whispers.

"Say it!" Jenny says.

Cynthia mumbles something no one could hear. I can see that her robe sash has come untied; her nightgown glowing beneath.

"Louder!" Jenny says.

Cynthia straightens up. "I told O'Connell," she says.

"What?"

"I told O'Connell!"

"What is the punishment for the crime?" Jenny calls out. Clearly this has all been rehearsed. Jenny and Missy H. bookends, black and white, yin and yang though far from balanced; the next year, after Missy H. wins the coveted Donaldson Thespian Prize at graduation, Jenny refuses to speak to her again.

Now Missy H. stands on the platform bench, raised above the rest of us, a candle she must have brought in her coat pocket beneath her chin, lit.

"Death by fright," she intones, lifting the candle high.

"What?" I say.

"Shh," Lucy says. "It's a game," she says.

Jenny spins Cynthia.

"This is what Trumbull does to Narks," she says, pushing her forward. Cynthia trips over the outer rail of the tracks, stumbling to the gravel ground. Then Jenny turns to the rest of us. "Hurry up," she says.

"What are we doing?" Fat Thomasina asks.

Jenny's blond hair glints beneath the streetlamp near the signal gate. "We're leaving," she says. "Hurry up." I watch her walking away, fast, Fat Thomasina trying to keep pace, the group's neat line dispersed but still following Jenny as she turns toward Carlton, Missy H. disappeared altogether from the platform, into the shadows. Cynthia has not moved from where she landed, on all fours, still blindfolded. In the settling silence a dog barks and she sits back, her hands covering her face as if it has not yet dawned on her that she is free to take off the bandanna to see where she is, or maybe it has and she does not want to look.

I take a step toward her. "Get up," I say but too quiet.

"Get up," I say again, louder.

And then the signal gate starts to swing down and the clanging begins and I step toward Cynthia but Lucy—still somewhere near—stops me. Give it a minute, she says, but I yell to Cynthia to get up. "Run," I yell, and she's trying but she keeps slipping on the gravel, still blind, and only then do I get my bearings and push past Lucy to Cynthia. (I would never have let anything happen, Lucy told me later. Who do you think I am?)

"I can do it," Cynthia's yelling. "Leave me alone. Get off of me," she's yelling, floundering and clawing at the bandanna and finally seeing and I do not know how much time passes before the train speeds by but not very much time at all. Cynthia, her knees and elbows skinned and bleeding from the gravel, her robe open now, the high collar of that ridiculous nightgown, is what I best remember. And how just then the speed of the train gone by feels like maybe it would be a better place to be—in that speed, in this dark, obliterated.

"It's okay," Lucy says. I am suddenly crying. "We wouldn't have let anything happen," Lucy says. "Jesus, Jo, don't be so dramatic. She talked to O'Connell about the North Woods. They busted a couple of seniors," Lucy says.

"You have to learn the rules," she says.

Cynthia moved home for good before the next semester, the spring semester, although spring semester at Hawthorne was still months of snow—January, February, March—and then April mud. May, during exams, or when you were packing to leave campus for the summer, brought the first hint of any weather that might make you want to stay, dogwood and forsythia, the thick, glorious lilacs that ringed the headmaster's house dangerous with bees, heady scented. Then mornings broke through the low, blank clouds and the dew that wet your boots, your sneakers, evaporated in an instant, or was siphoned, according to Lucy, who spent most of her time in my single, as interested in the better real estate I offered as in my friendship, I was aware, although I was about as close to her as I was to anyone then. I liked her unique way of looking at things.

Slim, the brilliant brother, had taught her that fairies lived in trees and under moss patches and that in the spring the reason the dew disappeared so fast in the mornings had to do with fairies harvesting the water. Slim's universe was magical for Lucy—she missed him terribly. He studied engineering at Cornell and though she and the rest of her family had always called him Slim at home, in their New York City apartment, he had recently written to her to say he would no longer answer to that—Frederic he preferred, a name, she told me, that meant nothing, her father's name.

That March she invited me home for the weekend; she still could not believe I had never been to New York City. Maybe that's why I appealed to her: my foreignness; the fact that Farmingdale High had been adjacent to a corn-field and the whole business about the flag twirlers and the Autumn Queen. "Tell me again about the Autumn Queen," she would say, out of the blue, the two of us trying to study in the first-floor lounge. "Did you think someday it might be you? Was that your highest aspiration? The foliage crown?"

"Miss Universe," I said. "My dream was always Miss Universe."

Her apartment building had a doorman who drove the elevator and a doorman who stood at the door waiting to open the door, something I found comical—those heavy coats and hats, the way he called her Miss Nightingale instead of Lucy, even though she called him Peter.

Slim, or Frederic, was home for that weekend as well. When we walked in, I handed him the daisies I had brought for Mr. and Mrs. Nightingale. He bent low and sniffed, he

was very tall and had to stoop, his eyes raccoon circled—
engineering, Lucy said. "Daisies," he said to me, smiling.
"The cheapest flower." Then he nodded at Lucy and turned
toward the kitchen, where the maid put the daisies still in
their green tissue paper in a glass meant for water.

They stayed there on the counter until we left on Sunday; Mr. and Mrs. Nightingale somewhere else for the
weekend and Slim, or Frederic, always out as well, with
his friends from Hawthorne who were home from their
various colleges, and an ex-girlfriend, Mary, we glimpsed as
the two passed through the Nightingales' ninth-floor living
room on their way to his bedroom, Lucy rolling her eyes.

"He broke up with her last summer," she said. "What
a douchebag." She turned again to the movie, one of a
handful of films whose titles blend together now, bands of
teenagers known at the time, recognizable, then lifted the
remote to click off the television set.

"Let's get stoned," she said.

And so we did, and then we called and ordered Chinese
food, near 2:00 A.M., and after that we went outside and
walked along the low stone wall that bordered Central Park,
and I thought of the Old Stone Wall Road and my mother's
retelling of the Colonel's patient explanation, and how far I
was from Farmingdale and the Huntington course, and the
look of Stephanie in the dark, staring toward me, already
unseeing, her neck snapped, and I almost told Lucy about
her, and I almost told Lucy about Master, who the weekend

before, at the spring dance, had walked out the side door with Charlotte P., turning to smile at me as he went, to blow a kiss, but then I did not. It was all too much to say aloud, to admit to anyone.

I bit my fingernail instead and held my nose and said, "What the hell?" and Lucy said, "I know. There's a freaking zoo, in Central Park," and I looked at the clock tower and I looked at the bare trees and I stopped to sit on one of the wood-slatted benches and put my head between my legs, breathing in the way I sometimes had to breathe and said, "I'm wasted."

I did not think of what my mother had written to me, how she had seen Carly's mother and that Carly's mother had been unkind. I did not think of Stephanie's brother, Buddy, laughing at her funeral and turning to find me, to smile at me, the person who had so many times before joined him in thinking something was funny. I did not think of anything but the feel of my breath, in and out, and how sitting this way, my head between my legs, was like I was in my own little cave, dark and warm, alone.

Here's the other thing about Buddy. He always told the truth, as if he had signed the upper-right corner of the paper of life. Stephanie and I used to put this to good work—when one of us really wanted a straight answer about an outfit, or hairstyle, we would find Buddy for his opinion.

You look ugly, he said to Stephanie after a particularly disastrous home permanent from a box we picked up at Whitman's. I had told her she looked fine. Different, I said, but fine.

Fine? she said.

Good fine, I said. Better than fine, fine. You know, just different fine. Hard-to-get-used-to fine. You know, I said.

She sat in front of Barbara the Nurse's master bathroom mirror and I stood behind her, the dregs of the permanent spread around us, plastic bag and gloves, empty bottle of chemical liquid we said must be safe or they would not include it. We had opened the window for the stench.

It's awful, she said. We both looked at her.

It's not, I said, taking the brush to brush again, thinking the brush's path would magically restore Stephanie's hair to Stephanie's hair, because right now Stephanie's hair looked like a wiry wig, the kind the lunch lady wore at Farmingdale High, and despite my hard brush strokes, it immediately sprang up, frizzy, clown-like, ridiculous.

"Buddy!" Stephanie yelled. He was always nearby when we were at her house, often lying in the hallway, waiting for us to come out of one room or another. Sometimes she would tell him to stop eavesdropping and sometimes she would ask him what he heard and make him swear not to tell the Colonel or Barbara the Nurse, which he swore, and you could count on that, and once in a while she would tell him if he wanted he could follow us into her room, or the master bathroom, where we practiced our makeup in the mirror or went through Barbara the Nurse's clothes hanging in the closet off the master bathroom, Stephanie's family far wealthier than mine, the Colonel having come from money, and Barbara the Nurse, inexplicably, in possession of glamorous formal wear.

Buddy stood at the bathroom door, his white button-down shirt, required for the special school he attended, untucked, his feet bare. He might have been twelve.

"What?" he said.

"How do I look?" she said.

He looked at her and bit his lip, a habit. "Ugly," he said.

"Ugly ugly?" she said.

Buddy nodded.

"Butt ugly," he said, and then he smiled his beautiful, sweet smile and shrugged, the three of us looking at the three of us in the mirror before we all started laughing. And then we laughed and laughed because it was funny. For a good long time in the mirror we watched ourselves, laughing.

I missed Buddy like hell after I killed Stephanie. I wanted to stand in front of Buddy and hear him speak his judgment of me, the truth. I wanted to hear him call me a murderer. But I never saw Buddy again after he turned to find me during the church service. Someone must have taken him home before the rest of us traveled to the cemetery and the grave, before all those people gathered outside in the rain. And after that the entire family packed up and moved to North Carolina to be near Stephanie's aunt and uncle. Where they went from there I never heard.

Spring at Hawthorne meant spring sports, when it seemed as if the entire school congregated in the gymnasium every afternoon, the boys on the lacrosse teams and the baseball teams and the track teams pounding clockwise around the upper-level track in gym shorts and Hawthorne-issue T-shirts or jerseys, the girls on the lacrosse teams and the softball teams and the track teams on the lower track, running counterclockwise, their own uniforms striped Hawthorne jumpers. Other groups clustered on the polished gymnasium courts, listening as coaches shouted drills above the reverberating din of balls smashing into the grilles protecting the fluorescent lights overhead, and the laughter and shouting, and the thud thud thud of the runners.

I returned to the weight room in the gymnasium basement, weight rooms then not like weight rooms now—no elliptical machines or Stair Masters, just some treadmills, a few rowing machines we were allowed to use after the crew boys had breezed through, and some rudimentary contraptions involving weights and bars and levers to pull or push, along with the requisite barbells and two- and five-pound weights stacked in racks against the mirrored back wall, already smeared with sweat by the time the group of us straggled in, around four o'clock, for our required hour.

Hawthorne's athletic director had gotten wise to the absurdity of independent training and so required anyone not on a team to be in a more formal weight-training class supervised by Billy, a long-haired misanthrope newly married to the girls' lacrosse coach, Leslie Bart, a legend at Dartmouth. We were as you can imagine a collection of oddballs: the Stubell twin brothers, piano prodigies terrified of damaging their hands; a little person, Karen, from St. Louis, with a wide, round face and tiny nose who from what I could observe took her height in stride—I never saw her outside the weight room without her boyfriend, Brett, the two of them draped over one another every time you turned a corner—and Parker, a Boston Brahmin Deadhead who smelled of patchouli and weed and fried food from his job at the Tuck Shop.

The rest outside of Alex I cannot remember—although I can picture the group of us, reflected in those mirrors on that first day, listening to Billy drone on. We did not warrant a coach, he was telling us, only a proctor who would clock our hours, sign our time sheets, and generally protect us from killing ourselves on these machines. Don't kill yourselves on these machines, Billy said. You could kill yourselves on these machines, Billy said. Don't be fooled, Billy said, these machines could kill you.

R-r-run for your l-l-life, Alex said. He stood a little apart from our group. Everyone knew him on campus for his patrician lineage, although despite this easy entrée to popularity he usually seemed to be alone, shoulders hunched, a bike messenger's bag strapped across his back. His mother was descended from French royalty and had married the king of some small country, Alex's surname unpronounceable, especially for poor Billy, who clearly did not give a rat's ass anyway. I later tell Alex he is straight out of Dostoevsky but now, the first time this close, I just look. He is exotic but not in an especially handsome way—more in a way that suggests a collection of furs in mothballs in a train trunk, heavy-lidded eyes, thick hair, a four o'clock beard, or maybe just a winter beard.

The first class is on a cold day in early January, and the weight room is steamy, oppressive. Billy asks Alex to repeat his name, clearly not having been apprised of Alex's lineage, or the story known to everyone about Alex's mysterious illness, brought on by an insect bite, I've been told, an illness as unpronounceable as his surname but one that fells him every few months and requires Alex to be excused from his classes and chauffeur driven to Boston, where he remains until he regains his health, or as much of his health as there is to be regained, and then returns to campus. Also the stutter, although there were fewer speculations about that—it was fairly constant and one of the reasons why, people assumed, Alex never talked much.

Everyone knows this, I want to tell Billy, who has proposed to Alex that maybe he would prefer going out for one of the teams instead of standing in Billy's weight room being a smart-ass. We all wait for what Alex will say next. Alex has the reputation of being someone who would say something next, who did not give a damn given his life sentence, maybe, or maybe because he was technically a prince.

"S-s-sorry, Billy," Alex says.

In off-hours, I have seen Billy in a maintenance uniform shoveling snow, and I have seen Billy in the mailroom handing out boxes and thick envelopes to those students lucky enough to have an orange postal slip, and I have seen Billy driving a snow plow, and I have seen Billy dishing out baked ziti in the dining hall, a plastic shower cap tightened around his tucked-up long hair. Billy known to everyone as, simply, Billy and generally liked and joked around with in the way the boys joke around with certain staff members, smacking his hand in a high five when they pass. Many of the boys do this, but not Alex, I imagine.

"Weights can kill you," Billy says, again.

"I u-u-u-understand," Alex says. "I c-c-c-completely get it, man."

"I'm glad to hear," Billy says. He starts passing out a mimeographed sheet of beginning rotations as he explains that he is passing around a mimeographed sheet of beginning rotations. Alex catches my eye and mouths "asshole." I smile and he smiles and we are suddenly partners in the idiocy of the apparatus: the silver machines with their pulleys and levers and hard seats and pins and blocks of varying weights, the diagrams with the arrows, the sounds of the track team just arrived to swarm the rowing machines— "we'll get to those last," Billy says. "Athletes have priority," Billy says, leading the group of us, the twin pianists and Karen and Parker and the rest of the assortment of boys and girls who have never been able to make a team, boys reed thin sprouted to a height they never imagined and girls with no depth perception, their knees banging the basketball court, swollen, iced, following Billy to hear again the increments of weight that may give them muscle mass and tone, that may turn them into something more for next time, because maybe next time they could be up there with the pounding runners and uniformed classmates.

This is a tangent, I know, and I apologize. Still, I think Alex may be the reason that I survived Hawthorne, despite even Lucy's friendship. Alex, who rolls his eyes and says that at least we will have checked off our sports requirement with this bullshit class, although Master would warn against the use of the future perfect—who can ever predict an act completed? Relegated to the past?

Alex, who suggests I apply to live in the International House off campus my junior year. This is where he planned to live, far away from the urban assholes. People who speak English as a second language are nicer, he said. Did I know he didn't stutter in French? Latinate rocks Germanic, he said.

It's all just sound anyway, he said. W-w-words.

I cannot say I was surprised to hear from Charlotte P. all these years later, that voice I would never not recognize, a beautiful voice, melodious, gentle.

In Modern Lit, she always spoke her opinions very softly, sotto voce, Master once said.

Gentlemen, he said. Note Fräulein Charlotte's strategy, sotto voce. Used by many shall we say well-endowed women you may bump into in life, pun intended: the translation? Speak softly and carry a couple of big sticks.

The boys laughed. Charlotte P. looked at me—maybe I smiled, maybe I laughed too. I was not sure what to do. Master's eyes were hard. Opaque. Certain times you had to choose sides and it seemed he no longer loved her. Just as well, since Charlotte P. would graduate at the end of the semester. Maybe he loved me now. Perhaps he loved me. His last letter he signed, Love, Christopher.

Another time, after mid-terms, we drive to the Forgotten Park, a picnic in the narrow back of the Alfa Romeo, a six-pack of beer and some cheese and crackers; this a Sunday. Master has waited for me in the Depot parking lot, the top rolled down. I see him on my way out the door. He is grading bluebooks, he says.

"What drudgery," he says, shoving them behind the seat. "Except yours, of course. You will pass with flying colors. You will pass with a fucking rainbow."

He drives fast, Jethro Tull on the eight-track, loud. He wears a baseball cap and his Princeton T-shirt and a windbreaker and promises later he will show me how to drive a stick shift if I promise I will sit in his lap as he shows me. My hair whips around, catches in my mouth, crazy. He yells above the wind that he would be delighted to teach me some other things as well.

He parks in the empty lot and jumps out. "My liege," he says, bowing, taking my hand to help me out too. The door sticks. The body is rusted. The automobile is a Grade A lemon but one he has had since he learned to drive and there are certain sentimental attachments. Plus, he has been a car freak since birth.

"Brian too?" I ask.

"Brian?" he says. He is reaching for the picnic. "Oh God, Brian. No," he says. He puts the basket on the parking lot ground, hard dirt. Spent cigarettes and bottle caps.

"Definitely not Brian," he says.

* * *

There are four other girls in Modern Lit besides Charlotte and me, although they are not his favorites. We are still his favorites. The others are smeared, their edges blurry, bleeding into the background, dissolved around the seminar table. I barely see them. And he pays little mind. Susan Cunningham raises her hand.

"Yes, Susan?" he says. "In sotto voce, please," he says. "Show the boys how it's done." Susan Cunningham lowers her hand. I notice Charlotte P. drawing a series of circles on her empty notebook page, blue-inked circles that get smaller and smaller, her pen digging into the paper.

"I'm sorry?" Susan says.

"In sotto voce," he says. "Like this," he whispers.

"Why?" Susan says.

"Because I said so," Master says. "You're illustrating by *example*," he says. "Nota bene."

Susan sits for a moment. She wears a suit that day—she must have been on her way after class to one of the on-campus college interviews for seniors—and the kind of tie popular with businesswomen at the time, half bow tie, half something else, not an especially flattering look for anyone but certainly not for Susan, whose hair hangs lank over her eyes and whose cheeks are scarred by acne, an atypical girl for Master's Modern Lit, yet everyone knows Susan is the smartest person at Hawthorne, so how could she have been denied? Now she sits mute, staring out at all of us as if looking for the right answer, or a different answer, since nothing makes sense. Understand Susan is a girl who usually speaks in perfect paragraphs, complete with introduction, thesis, and conclusion, air quotes, often a girl so excited by what she has to say, by what she *believes*, that she sits on her hands, confessing once to the class that she knows her habit of gesticulating is annoying, and so that's why.

Did anyone in here say it was annoying? Master had said. I find it sweet.

"Never mind," Susan whispers now.

Master walks over to stand behind her, placing a hand on either padded shoulder. "Cat got your tongue?"

"I forgot what I wanted to say," she says.

"Happens to the best of you," he says, winking at us from behind Susan. "But don't you look lovely," he adds.

Charlotte P. and I talked on the telephone for a while. Then she told me you were looking for corroboration and that's why she had called. She said she thought I would want to tell you my story as well.

It is not an understatement to say it shocked me to hear; you may find it hard to understand, but the details she brought up about herself felt both true and foreign, like reading the story of a parallel me, one who has stood just a little to the side, someone whom I have forced to live outside my own life for so long she feels like a phantom twin.

I understand for your purposes I will remain anonymous and be referred to as Student A, or Student B or C. I also understand that the details of my story, like Charlotte P.'s, must be corroborated, this entire judiciary exercise like stacking *matryoshka*, those Russian nesting dolls, corroboration within corroboration, nothing too quickly, or readily, believed. We girls like to make shit up, right?

Besides, years have flowed into years and students and teachers have given way to students and teachers. Master not the only one. I imagine several headmasters dismissed accounts as nothing more than passing infatuations—a stolen kiss, inappropriate innuendo—although some took them more seriously. In certain incidents, I have heard, fathers were called in, fathers assumed better capable of confronting the embarrassment of the parties involved or the complexities of what it meant for the accused men, some fathers irate, some going along with the euphemisms, the excuses, the understandable subtleties of living in such close proximity.

In other cases mothers came too, although these were fewer and usually only when legal action was threatened. The result was emergency meetings and forced resignations, both parties agreeing to mum's the word, the accused moving on to the next school, preferably a boys' school, a well-considered recommendation letter from the headmaster or dean of faculty in hand, one that tightroped the boundary of the admittedly tricky boundaries, the words carefully chosen: This one might err on the side of *fraternity*, the headmaster wrote. This one likes to *consort* with students, he wrote. All quickly forgotten once out of sight.

But there were also those who stayed on, men who may have been given a rebuke or called in for questioning—someone had seen them at the semiformal, dancing with X, someone had noticed Y in their car after the game, was it true? they were asked.

Truth is relative, they might have said. Yes and no, they might have said. You know girls and their imaginations, they might have said.

These teachers remained, Master among them, although eventually he returned to Madrid, a voluntary early retirement, his many distinctions through service to the English Department, coaching teams, and proctoring Dunewood House, crowned with Hawthorne's Jameson Teaching Award, its highest faculty honor. At the award ceremony, testaments from past students whose lives he forever changed, students who would never read Dickens, or Yeats, or Shakespeare, or Wallace Stevens without remembering his brilliant recitations, his insights, his wit, were read aloud to the gathered by Teddy Pyle, now head of Alumni Affairs.

So corroboration, I understand, is needed. Corroboration is what you have asked for, though I imagine that each of us favorites must have her own version of Master, or Master Aikens, or M, the narrative shifting depending on the storyteller, the year, the season, the angle of light: Memory, as you may recall, is a revision of a revision of a revision, the fortieth draft, or the forty-first.

For instance, I might have used an entirely different perspective—third-person omniscient, or I might have left out Buddy, or Alex, or even Lucy, certainly the business of the daisies—why mention daisies in green tissue paper shoved into a glass meant for water? What do daisies on a kitchen counter—the maid returned to the chair where she sat for the rest of the day reading her Bible—have to do with this story? Or maybe I would have included more of Cynthia, the way I went to say goodbye, the two of us since the night of the train tracks having barely spoken a word to one another. Her mother had flown in, her grandmother too, a kind-looking, white-haired lady in a wool suit and good pumps I would later see standing on the South Woods path, her old hands clasped behind her, looking down as if for a penny. Cynthia left school as abruptly as I arrived: a Friday morning, the rest of the girls in classes.

I helped her pack or did not help her pack. She wanted nothing to do with me. Her mother folded clothes and blankets and Cynthia took down those posters of the opera stars whose names I never learned, the hang-in-there cat poster, boxed her record albums, her collection of favorite books, *The Loneliness of the Long-Distance Runner* one I should have read earlier and finally did in one sitting in a public library far away from Hawthorne.

Always the conditionals, Master said. Would haves, should haves, could haves: nothing claimed, nothing asserted.

Or maybe I would tell it from his perspective.

He speaks of the fluid definitions between a boy and a man. Explains that he was a late bloomer, like Wallace Stevens, just out of graduate school, an idiot: a young boy at heart lacking the maturity and self-control to be surrounded by so many very young, very pretty, girls, especially the impressionable ones, and let's be honest, they were *all* impressionable. Like shooting fish in a barrel. And needy and, well, they went along, didn't they? Each of them went along. He never forced himself on anyone, he says, and if there was involuntary consent it was consent nonetheless, in a manner of speaking. It is always a manner of speaking, isn't it? He said/she said.

Those were different times! The faculty were told by the administration to get to know the students, to take them out and listen to their predictable horror stories of home—alcoholic parents, bullying brothers, neurotic mothers, distant fathers. They were encouraged to sympathize, empathize, soothe. Those girls had *problems*. And who can say why or when a buoying hug or gesture of some kind might lead to more?

Aren't we all after the same thing? The human connection? The warmth?

But here is where I draw the line. Here is where I stop him. Declarative.

No, I say. In no moral universe would this not be a crime, I say.

I was a child, I tell him.

There is right and there is wrong.

Shame on you, I say. Shame on you, I say. Shame on you.

And he laughs and reaches out for me.

"You are cute as pie when you're angry," he says.

"Come here," he says.

"How old are you again?" he says.

"Close your eyes," he says.

The magnolia grew at the edge of our yard, a gift from some friends of my parents with whom they were quite close around the time I was born—my parents a lot of fun then, partyers who waited a long time for me, as some parents do for children. Anyway, these friends made a fuss about my birth and on the day I was born they went to our house and planted the tree at the edge of our yard, a dwarf magnolia, to surprise my parents when they returned from the hospital. And because of the Maryland soil or the light or God knows what, the magnolia kept growing and growing, the joke in our family that the poor tree did not know its own dwarf limitations, that it thought anything was possible and so reached that majestic height as if planted from a magic seed, its leaves wide and glossy, sometimes a dark green and sometimes almost black. It blossomed the most glorious white blossoms, saucer shape, fragrant. Our magnolia too big for its britches, my father said. A show-off.

The point is, before everything, before I grew up, before I killed her, before Hawthorne and Master, before Carly, even, when Stephanie and I were just kids, on afternoons my mother had stepped out, which were most afternoons, we would climb the magnolia's sturdier branches, daring each other to get to the next, to reach the top, where a particular one we had tested would still be there, we knew, because it was a tree, and its branches were where its branches were supposed to be, and we knew it could hold both of us for as long as we wanted and as long as neither one of us ever looked down. Looking down spelled doom. We had to look up at the clouds, or the vista of the green course or the players moving around the fairways.

Look at that, we would say. And we would look, talking about God knows what, nothing and everything, how she planned on becoming a veterinarian, and how I planned on becoming a poet, and how the two of us might move to New York and live together after college for a year or two, the air fresh so high we were giddy from it, or maybe we were just kids, grass-stained knees, bone and blood, our possibilities endless, life endless, friendship endless, she and I endless, never ending, never ever, never ending.

And somewhere far away the sorry magpie sang, Sorry, sorry, sorry, sorry, sorry.

Or, from a different perspective:

The young girls sit high in the thick of the magnolia

talking. They are difficult to see so high among its shiny green and black leaves, but know they are there, full of grace, beautiful, inching out on a limb they believe would not dare to break beneath the weight of them.

O, the weight of them.

The weight of us.

ACKNOWLEDGMENTS

Many thanks to the generous friends who read early drafts of this novel and offered invaluable insights: Lynne Guillot, Polly Edelson, Cliff Cunningham, Aria Beth Sloss, Lindsay Whalen, Dorothy Wickenden, Roxanne Coady, and Carolyn Cooke. For enlightening conversation, heartfelt thanks to Laura Barr and Kim Hurd. For their brilliance and tenacity, I'm deeply grateful to Nan Graham and Eric Simonoff. Thank you also to Mia Crowley-Hald, Tamar McCollom, and Katie Monaghan.